LEVELS

D H RICHARDS

A QUANTA BOOK

an imprint of Shirtsleeve Press

Published by Shirtsleeve Press

Dallas, Texas

CHAPTER ONE

The crime scene was pretty unremarkable. The dead man who lay behind the small counter—neck blown out, an array of blood splattered behind him—had contracted Talbot before, offering simple collection work for deadbeat credits.

The small shop was in the jewelry district. It was no more than 10 feet wide and, with the back room, only about 20 feet deep. Two beat cops milled nervously around the dead man.

The family must have called me right after they called the cops, Talbot thought as he took in the scene. No sign of a break in…the dead man knew the shooter. The glass cases were intact, nothing stolen. It looked like a hit. Talbot was about to ask what detective was assigned when she walked in the door.

You could always tell Protocol Dicks: they dressed better and had an air of simultaneous boredom and superiority about them. He could see right away she was not from Level 29; her demeanor was all Protocol. She scanned the place and focused on one of the beat guys.

"Ricky," she said offhandedly, "go get the kit from Officer Kinderman's mobile."

"Uh, that's Kinderweiss…"

She did not register the man's objection. "And also have him call the coroner. And you, out, no civilians, this is a sealed area." The woman had turned to look at Talbot, who was standing to the left of the front door.

"I'm not a civilian, detective."

"Who are you then?"

"I represent the family of the deceased. I'm here to make sure the department does its best to find the man's kill—"

"You the polish, eh?"

Talbot smiled a wide grin. The polish was not a 29 term.

"You're not local department are you?" he asked trying to sound casual but inwardly bracing for a fight. "Upper levels I would say…35–36?"

"Thirty-four. How did you know?"

Talbot smiled again; he had overestimated the level on purpose. He had assumed 33 or even 32 but was glad he'd overshot a little. Nothing like a little compliment to get off on the right foot with the detective.

"Down here we're called the assist; the polish is upper level. Also, your clothes…"

She momentarily looked concerned, "What about them?"

Talbot filed that away: she was concerned with her appearance but not vain, just wanted to be sure she looked the part. Talbot eyed her up and down briefly. She had the trim look of a woman in her early thirties, petite but not especially short—five feet six or seven, he figured. Her brown hair was styled with salon quality and she wore a crisp suit that showed off her body but not in a suggestive or trampy way. Her appearance reflected control and precision. This he could work with.

"They're a couple credits above what the average person 'round here can afford."

"Look, Mr...."

"Singh, Talbot Singh," he smiled and offered his hand.

She shook it perfunctorily. "Mr. Singh, you need to leave. Or at least go onto the street. I can assure you this case is in good hands."

"No doubt, Detective...?"

"Detective Olson."

"I promise to not interfere."

"It's not a request Mr. Singh. Out—now."

"Detective—"

"If you don't go I will ask Officer Kinderbody to escort you out."

"Kinderweiss can vouch for me."

"Mr. Singh," any attempts at civility had left her voice, "now!"

"Okay, leaving. Only, don't be mad at me when you realize the huge mistake you've made," he shrugged, betting she was someone who hated to make mistakes and the lack of control mistakes presumed.

She opened her mouth and then closed it, a hesitant look crossing her eyes. "What mistake is that, exactly?"

"The victim," he nodded toward the man slumped against the wall behind the counter. "He's holding a playing card."

"Okay."

"A gang hit."

"Which one? I thought 29 was pretty free of gang activity."

"Gangs, yes. Activity, not so much. It's not this level, probably lower."

"Which one?"

"Ahhhh, well," Talbot smiled again, prompting a deep frown from the detective. "You see that is where I can be of service. I have...I wouldn't say friends, but people I know down in lower levels."

"How low?"

"Twenty-five...24...even 19."

"Great, thanks. I'll take that into consideration. I can get our gang activity people to look it up."

"How long will that take? A week? More?"

"Perhaps, not that it—"

"I can get it to you tomorrow morning, the latest."

"Mr. Singh, you need to leave. Kinder... Kinder guy!"

"No need to blow, Detective. I'll go. Just be careful. I know this may look like just another hit—"

"And why wouldn't it be?" She held her hand up to stop Kinderweiss, who looked at Talbot and rolled his eyes in annoyance.

"Sloppy work. They broke the window and the lock, the victim was going for a weapon. All pointing to a perfectly normal crime scene." Talbot picked up the playing card, turning it over in his hand. "Except..."

"What's wrong Mr. Singh?"

Talbot looked up at the posh detective from level 34.

"You. You, Detective, are all wrong."

Olsen tilted her head as if looking at a strange bird in a cage.

"Go on," she smiled slightly.

"What are you doing here, all the way down on this level? My guy here, the dead guy? He's good people. Been running this store for 20 years, never any problems—probably because what he sells is low-rate junk, but still. And now he gets hit and instead of some third shift decker, they send Ms. Uptown herself. I'm not trying to make trouble, Detective, but so far this whole thing just reeks of something."

Detective Olsen did not say anything, she just held out her hand to take back the card. Talbot held it back, his eyes questioning.

She sighed. "Orders from above my pay grade Mr. Singh. Turns out the super's daughter goes to school with his granddaughter or something."

"A climber, huh? Who knew?"

"What's wrong with climbing?" Olsen bristled.

"Nothing, especially if it gets you upper-level deckers down on low-level jobs like this." Talbot replied absently, focused on using his watch to scan the playing card's back. He looked up to see Olsen's curious expression. "Cards are coded, by gang, by time." Talbot explained. "I should be able to tell you who left this, or at least the folks someone wants you to think left it."

Olsen's eyes narrowed. "You really can get that by tomorrow?"

"Sure, probably. Have to go down to 19 but, you know, might be a bit of fun sightseeing down there."

Olsen gave a small hollow laugh. "Braver than me. Here, Mr. Singh."

"Friends call me Talbot."

"Yes, well…Here—my card." She tapped her watch. Talbot

9

felt his watch ding, signaling receipt. "Use it to come up tomorrow."

"This'll pay?"

"Yes, it's a pass. One time," she added with a warning in her voice.

"What about my fare up from 19?"

"What about it? You want play with the big boys then pony up Mr. Singh," Olsen said.

"Right."

"You ever been up beyond here?" Olsen asked.

"Once. Family vacation to 32 when I was eight. It was about the same, if you ask me."

Olsen looked around and shrugged. "Yeah, 34's pretty much like this."

"How far you been up, Detective?"

"Forty," she replied. "Same as you: little vacation."

"They say there's a park on 40."

"Yes, went there."

"And? Did you see any of it? The sky?"

She shrugged. "Could have seen it, not sure. If I did it was very far away, maybe another… what, 10 levels?"

"I hear the city is up to 70 total now."

Olsen made a noncommittal noise. "Well, Mr. Singh, if you find anything see me tomorrow. Don't call—security protocol, you know. And don't bother coming if you can't find anything. This is low priority."

"Sure, okay."

Olsen smiled tightly and then made a gesture towards the door.

"Oh, yeah, right. Pleasure, Detective." Talbot turned on his heel and left the small shop.

The little jewelry store did not sit on the street but rather in a small collection of shops set behind a glassed-in alcove with tables, chairs, and a small coffee stand. Passersby could and did walk by, oblivious to the police activity. But people from the neighborhood looked, and whispered to each other. They knew something had happened.

The man in the jewelry store was proprietor Jay Mill, a fixture in the area who sold affordable jewelry in plain boxes. Although many people frequented his tiny shop, few wanted to boast they actually bought trinkets from him; Mr. Mill did not barter in the high-end items. But he was friendly, outgoing, and, importantly, unpretentious. Talbot knew that people around the area did not take well to climbers: people who pretended to be better than they were.

The area was officially known as area 19 level 29, but most people called it Assembly. It's what people did there: worked in large assembly plants. They would take parts made elsewhere, usually on lower levels, and put them together, everything from large elevator engines to small, biostic takeout food boxes. The level was six stories tall—not luxurious, but tall enough. He knew from forays below that levels shrunk in height as you went down.

The level was well lit, reasonably clean, and the air—to his mind at least—fresh enough. It helped that level 28 had multiple air handling factories. Assembly was, in short, an unpretentious place that did not suffer pretentious people well.

Talbot had grown up on the level, part of a large family;

extended in all directions except for his. His mother and father still lived in the apartment he grew up in, but they never had any more children after he came along. He had cousins upon cousins but his family was always the small, three-person unit.

Despite the six-story buildings that rose all around him and that expanded outward for miles, space was at a premium. Seventy-four million people, give or take a few, lived on level 29. Mill's jewelry shop was small not just because it sold small items. Everywhere Talbot looked was crowded with people, goods, and buildings—but mostly people. He liked it this way. He could lose himself quickly in the crowds or just as quickly find people he knew. He had honed this ability over the past 10 years as a professional assist. And before that, as a young teenager he had helped Mr. Hammaud, a friend of the family who had also been an assist.

The job of an assist was simple: to make sure that when things happened to a family, those things went as well as could be expected. Strictly speaking he was not a lawyer or, to use a very old term, a fixer. Instead he...well, assisted families that could afford to hire him. When a family had one of their own get picked up by the police, he would be there to make sure the police did their job and the family member kept their mouth shut. If there was a dispute within the family or between families, he acted as the middleman, solving whatever issue had come up between them. He might have to help people get licenses to operate a business or help negotiate the purchase of an apartment—the latter always a tricky proposition.

Rarely did he have to represent a family in the case of death. Natural death was handled by the funeral houses. Only twice before had he interceded for murder, and in both cases it was domestic violence. And in both cases he represented the person who had done the killing. Mr. Mill was a different circumstance and Talbot had a small knot in the pit of his stomach because of it. He was in uncharted territory. He had learned early on that when facing the unknown, go slowly and carefully.

As he wandered the streets of Assembly's shopping district he considered what little he knew: Mr. Mill, a third-rate jewelry man, had been gunned down in his shop. The killing exhibited signs of a gang hit, down to the playing card left near Mr. Mill. Beyond those simple facts…Talbot had known Mr. Mill his whole life; the man had never caused even the smallest amount of trouble. Jewelers were often known to fence goods or pass through dirty credits so the fact that Mr. Mill was so clean was remarkable in and of itself—and a problem.

The presence of the 34th level detective was sending off loud sirens in Talbot's head. He had never seen one come down, unless, and here his mind snagged, unless they were investigating a crime in which the perp was from level 29, certainly not the victim. The connection that Olsen had offered rang hollow with Talbot. He made a mental note to speak with Mr. Mill's widow as soon as he could. He would not have pegged them—or more specifically, one of their children—as climbers.

Around noon, after grabbing a quick lunch of nasi, Talbot made his way towards the apartment he shared with his parents. He squeezed himself into the tiny elevator that rose up to the fifth floor. He smiled wryly each time he hit the number five button on the elevator. His father had often told the story of how they had initially been offered an apartment on the sixth floor, but he had turned it down, fearing that people would accuse him of being a climber by trying to get as close as he could to the 30th level.

As Talbot made his way into the apartment the lights inside flickered on. The apartment was large and well kept. The main room was a standard 10x10 foot with its entryway kitchen, the sofa bed where he slept, and the large panel screen on the wall. At the end of the room was a doorway into another 10x10 foot space that housed a bathroom and his parent's room, plus a small storage area. He grabbed a bottle of something fizzy and sweet from the fridge. He sat down at the small counter that separated the kitchen from the main room and punched up his father's number. Seconds later a small, gray-haired man with a neatly trimmed white beard flickered into view on the small screen hanging from the kitchen ceiling.

"Tal! Such news. I heard about Mr. Mill. Was it a robbery?"

"Hey, Pops. Not sure yet. Looks weird. I wanted to tell you that I have to go down a few levels this afternoon. I may not be back until after dinner."

The man on the screen, who was carefully pasting brightly colored paper into what seemed like a wooden book, looked up.

"How many?"

"Uh, well, you know…a few."

"How many?" His voice was steady but demanding.

"To 19, Pop."

"No."

Talbot sighed and tried to smile. "Pop, I'm not 10. I can handle myself. I need to ask a few guys questions is all."

"So this Mr. Mill was tied up in gangs?"

"I never said."

"No reason to go to 19 unless it's for gangs, Tal."

"Yeah, well…so anyway."

"You tell your mom yet?"

"Of course not, that's why I called you."

The old man did not smile; instead he stared for a moment at the screen and then bent back over his work. "Don't be a fool, Tal. See you after dinner then."

"Thanks, Pop."

Talbot ended the call and took a long sip of the drink. He knew his father was only being protective, but sometimes he wondered how it would be to live on his own. He was almost 30. He figured if he got married he could move out. Maybe. But that wasn't on the horizon right then. He could never afford to rent a place on his own—assuming he could find one. His parents had spent 35 years paying down on the one they lived in now. Well, he could always dream. Or find a new girlfriend.

CHAPTER TWO

Under the eternal orange-blue glow of the day-lights that tracked over each street, Talbot made his way to E-station 1138. The E stood for elevator, the main way around the city. Levels were connected by thousands of elevators. The system was pretty simple. It was always free to ride down; it was the ride up that cost. And the further you went up, the higher the cost. A ride up to 30 might cost the average person a day's wage. To get to 34 might cost half a year's wage. Vacation packages often helped to reduce the cost, but they also came with chip implants. When your vacation was done you had to ride back down, or the IIP—Internal Immigration Protocol—would track you down within minutes.

And even if one saved up wages to ride implant-free to the upper levels, living in the upper levels would be impossible. Not only was everything more expensive, jobs were impossible without the proper documents and scans. People did it all the time, but it took a concentrated effort. Often families would pitch in to send one member, often the brightest or most talented son or daughter, to school a level up hoping they could climb. Those left behind were almost always resentful, so the term climber was usually spat out of people's mouths.

Going down, however, was free and often too easy. Lose your job, gamble too much, run afoul of the protocols and you could find yourself settling down, moving a level or more down to escape debt or to find easier, less skilled work. Branches of families that settled down were often erased from collective memory and never mentioned, as if they had died. Going down was free and dangerously easy.

But like the vacations up, going down was not just one-way. Talbot loaded up a transit card with the credits he would need to come back from 19. For him the 10 levels would cost about half the fee he was charging the Mill family. But he figured it was an investment. He could find out about the card and then zip up to 34 to see Olsen. After that…well, the future was a bit cloudier. But he felt that the money spent would come back to him somehow. He chuckled; thinking like this was probably why he hadn't been able to save for his own place.

Talbot had picked the station on purpose. One of the older stations, it was a little shabby but bottomed out on 19 near where he needed to go. No sense landing blocks away and putting himself on those streets more than he needed to. No sense being a fool.

The doors to the elevator were open. The car, roomy with large glass windows, could easily hold 100 people. It had 10 rows of benches in the middle and benches all along the perimeter. He never understood the reason for the large windows. The only view going down or up was the concrete tube that held the lift rails. He guessed the large windows made it seem less claustrophobic.

It was midafternoon so the compartment was almost empty.

Large signs posted all around the station and in the compartment gave strict warnings about re-upping if needing credits on the transit app. Talbot checked his watch for the 100th time, looking to make sure the transit balance was still loaded.

He chose a seat on the perimeter and glanced up at the schedule. This particular lift was an express, only stopping at 24 before hitting 19. It was slowly filling with an assorted group of people. It was a midday crowd; Talbot knew that in the evening, when he hoped to return, the lift would be full of people coming back from work in the heavy metal factories on 19 and the heavy industry on 24. Most would be mid-level managers or salesmen checking up on production; few, if any, would be line workers.

The lift was not even a quarter full when the doors closed. The compartment shook slightly and began its descent. The ride down was almost comically anticlimactic for such a large moving room. It stopped with a small shudder at 24, where most people got out. The few people left studiously avoided making eye contact with each other. Within minutes they would dart out of the lift on 19 and make their way into a place few willingly went.

When Talbot left the lift and climbed up the short flight of stairs into the street he felt calm, almost at home. It was not his first time on 19. His mentor, Mr. Hammaud, seemed to have frequent business on the level. While not the sort of place one would want to linger in, 19 was not as bad as its reputation.

The level was home to smelting plants and chemical plants, the kind of dirty work that people on upper levels needed but did not want near them. Like those on 29, 24, or any level really, most people lived their lives free from drama or much crime. But unlike a level like 29, the attitude of the protocols was a bit more relaxed on 19. Although shrouded in myth, 19 was home to several of the better organized gangs, which were basically businesses that ran the goods society wanted and craved, but if you believed the moral authorities were not proper. From what Talbot knew, they supplied people on many levels, at least up to 29. They provided the drugs, code, mechs, and people that those who could afford to used.

But Talbot was not there to procure or even to judge; he just needed information and knew where to go. The man, another jeweler, was ensconced in a store possibly smaller than that of the deceased Mr. Mill. He was a large, fleshy man with a wheezing cough. Talbot had been introduced to him about 10 years earlier by Hammaud. Even then the man seemed as if he would seize up and die at any moment, but here he was 10 years on still wheezing and coughing, still alive.

Talbot pushed himself into the small store. He almost had to lean over the glass showcase in order to close the door behind him. The large man behind the case gave a hearty laugh, somewhat forced.

"Mr. Singh! What do I owe the pleasure? Come to shop for an engagement ring?"

Talbot was not sure why the man winked. Still, he forced out a smile, not wishing to get off on the wrong foot. "Strictly business, sorry to say." Glancing down at the cheap and gaudy trinkets in the case below he was really not sorry. "On a case."

"You work too hard, sir. This is why you are not here buying jewelry for some lucky bird, no?"

Talbot smiled, but another glance down made him shake his head.

"These are the finest rings, I wish you would let me show some instead of being so dreary with all of your business, Mr. Singh."

"Yes, well, my client has been murdered."

"No! Such a shame, murder. Never ends well for anyone involved, does it? But why are you down here bothering me? Was it a crime of passion? Did I sell her lover jewelry?"

Talbot gave a small laugh; someone might be driven to murder if they got one of the rings in the store as a gift. "No, he was a jeweler himself. But I think it was a hit."

"Ach, now that is bad. A hit? Why? Not a robbery?"

"This was left." Talbot projected an image of the card from his watch. It floated above the counter as the fleshy man leaned down to examine it.

"Huh, a calling card you think?" The jeweler propped himself back up, his expression inscrutable.

"Seems like. Seems like something one of the organizations from 19 might leave behind."

"Now, what would one of our local businesses want with a jeweler from 29?"

"That is the first of many questions, so I wanted to see if you could tell me which group this is from? Can you tell by the markings on the back?"

"Yes. Very clear. It is Treasure group, for sure. But strange still…"

"Treasure?" Talbot knew about them, but wanted to find out any information the jeweler might have on them.

"They move drugs mostly—narcs, alteragents. Why worry

with a jeweler. He a user?"

"Not that I know of. Plus if he was, why hit him? If he owed money that would be a local problem."

"I'm beginning to see why you have a lot of questions, Mr. Singh. But this is a little out of my area. I will send you to a man I know. A man who can confirm the card and also, perhaps, read the details."

"Oh yeah, I meant to ask—"

"I do not keep up enough to be able to read the backs, just the group signs." The man pushed a small card across the counter. Talbot looked surprised the jeweler didn't just tap the address to his wrist.

"Some things are best left off the electrical, Mr. Singh," he said with a wry smile. "This man, Mr. Geertz, should be able to help you. But I have to warn you, he is the suspicious type. Show him my card; perhaps that will help."

"Thank you." Talbot took the card and scanned the address. It was not in a place where he would normally go.

The man saw his look. "You'll be okay. With the factories around there will be many people in the streets. Now, when you do find that special lady, come back to me, I will give you a good price!"

Talbot left the small store with an uneasy feeling. It was already three in the afternoon. He knew that a level like 19 did not dim their lights but still, it would be unwise to stay too late. Once workers drifted back home or to other levels, the streets would be empty. So he took a deep breath and called up a projection map. It was another 10 blocks. A little far, but Talbot didn't mind walking.

Plus he felt safer in the streets than he would on a conduit line below.

As he walked Talbot marveled at how different, yet similar, this level was to 29. He remembered learning in school that two hundred years earlier 19 was the top level of what was then a metropolis of less than a billion. City planners had built a gaudy, luxurious level to celebrate the ever-burgeoning growth of their megacity. The only trouble was that within 25 years more levels had been added and the appeal of living on 19 faded quickly. The whole architecture of the city changed with 19. The level was only four stories high giving a cramped, oppressive feeling. After 19, planners built taller levels, with more stories for buildings. They also designed better lighting and better ventilation. The air in 19 was hot, sticky, the light overhead a sickly shade of yellow.

The buildings, faded and barely kept up, belied the level's once-grand status reflected in the ornate stone and plaster work, spacious entry ways, large front windows. Talbot wondered what the average apartment looked like. He had heard they were larger than those on 29. By the time the upper levels had been built it became more about packing people in than style. He often wondered what it would be like to try and get a place here, although he knew the tradeoff of having to live on 19 would not be worth the larger living space.

Most of the residents he passed seemed threadbare and haggard. The bad air and pale light wore on people. Talbot knew the factories here were not as modern or pleasant, if that was the word, to work in as those on 29. The materials handled—heavy metals, caustic chemicals, and a decided lack of the most up-to-date mechs—meant people came into contact with the killing material. Most people here lacked other opportunities, or rather, other legitimate opportunities. They could sink to even lower levels or they could turn to crime. Running illegal goods was dangerous but plausibly less fatal than handling lethal chemicals and poisonous metals.

Hustling down the dingy streets, Talbot made good time to the address the man had given him. It was a grey building with large smoky windows and a curiously small entryway. Elaborate plaster sculptures graced each side of the door, the chipped and worn faces of long forgotten Hindi gods and goddesses. Equally chipped and faded gold lettering on the door announced it was the home of Cultural Imports and Exports, Inc. Talbot pushed his way through the heavy glass door into a cramped foyer. A small elevator sat to the side.

It made Talbot nervous that he had to go up to the third floor. He would be off the street, a quick exit denied. He made a mental note of where the stairs were. He wondered if they were blocked or not. No one was in the lobby area. The building almost seemed deserted and it was only around 4 p.m.—another strange sign. He pushed the elevator call button. The compartment was almost as small as the one in his apartment building. He felt trapped during the short trip up.

It was with some relief that he got out of the tiny space. But his relief was short lived. The building was getting increasingly strange. He began to realize the lack of people was no accident; few businesses would willingly set up shop here. The ceilings were low, barely above his six-foot frame. The lights were low, making it difficult to see numbers on the doors that lined the short hallway.

He found the door he was looking for tried the handle. Not surprisingly, it was locked. Talbot knocked. A moment later the door opened a sliver revealing a tall, thin man with solid black hair and red eyes. He said nothing while looking Talbot up and down. When he began to close the door, Talbot stuck his foot in the frame.

"Are you Geertz? I have this card. I was told you might be able to help me."

The man took the card, glanced at it, and handed it back. "What is it you want?" His voice was just above a whisper.

"Uhm, I have a card…a playing card. I'm told you might be able to tell me about the markings."

The door swung open and Talbot cautiously eased in. The man was already walking away toward a small desk set against the window on the opposite wall. The room was large, cavernous even, but aside from the desk and the chair completely empty. The man stopped at the desk, which was also bare, and turned around. He was wearing a long, black leather coat, buttoned up against a slight chill in the room. Talbot wondered why he didn't simply adjust the room's conditioning.

"Show me what you have."

Talbot made his way across the room and with a flick projected the card in front of the man. The card's red back shimmered in the light. For the first time Talbot could swear he saw the minute red markings making up the elaborate design actually move.

"Treasure, but you knew that, even the jeweler you saw can read that. Where is this from?" Geertz tilted his head at the projection, a slight smile on his face.

"It was found on 29. On the body of my client."

The man's eyebrows raised. "You a protocol?"

"Talbot Singh, assist for the family of the deceased."

"Go on."

"Mr. Mill ran a small jeweler's booth. Quiet type, kept his nose clean. Found this morning shot in the head and neck. The card was on his chest."

"Was the store robbed?"

"No. Mostly cheap stuff, but nothing you'd leave if you meant to rob. It was made to look like a gang hit."

"Made? You seem uncertain. There is this card, after all."

"Yes, there is some other stuff, nothing much," Talbot lied, not wanting to give away too much too soon, "It just seemed odd that a group from 19 would hit a guy like my client."

"Groups here do business up there, as I'm sure you know."

"But they don't normally hit. They let locals do that work… usually."

"You said the hit was this morning?"

"Overnight I guess, early morning."

The man glanced down at the card floating in space and then back up to Talbot. "Mr. Singh, either you are an accomplished liar or a fool."

"I can assure you I'm neither Mr. Geertz," Talbot said crisply.

"Well, no fool at least, although you deigned to come down to our level."

"Not my first time here, I know what."

"No need to establish cred with me, Mr. Singh. I'm not sure what game this is or for that matter who is even playing, but I suspect you are a pawn and about to get trounced on by a stronger piece."

"Why? What's wrong with the card? Is it fake or is it real?"

"Real enough, although not real and certainly not correct. This card you are showing me is over a year old. It's possible that it would have been used as recently as six months ago, but not this morning, not by a Treasure."

"You sure?"

"Of course."

"How?"

"I designed it, Mr. Singh. Now, why don't you tell me what is really going on here?"

"I told you what I know, Mr. Geertz." Talbot let out a deep breath. He tried to quell a rising sense of panic he felt rising from his stomach. "Look, I think you are right. Maybe I'm a pawn here. Someone is playing with this case. None of this adds up. Maybe it's another group, trying to throw off the scent." Talbot knew he was fishing, if only Geertz would bite.

"No, not another group. They wouldn't be able to make this card—or at least make it this right."

"Then who?"

"You tell me, Assist. Who has the ability to know about and make something this correct and yet out of date?"

Talbot's mind raced. If not a gang then only protocol would be able to.

"Hey, wherever you're leaping to, I'm not there, Mr. Geertz. I don't get involved with protocol matters. Never have. I think it's best for me to go now."

"No, stay. I think I want you to meet some people." Geertz flicked his wrist to reveal a small watch. Talbot did not wait to see what was next. As fast as he could he turned on his heels and bolted for the door.

Making it out into the hallway he saw a door at the end of the hall begin to open. He quickly made his way down to the other end to where he hoped there were stairs. It took two pushes, a light one and then one with full body force, before Talbot was able to get the stairway door to open. As he suspected, the stairwell was full of garbage, discard furniture, old electronics. Grabbing the rail guides, he swung himself down the flights of stairs as fast as he could. He was already on the second floor when he heard the door he'd just pushed his way through burst open. He heard a voice shouting for him to stop.

He went faster.

Within seconds he threw himself down the last flight of stairs, still swinging on the guide rails over the piled junk. A side exit door was remarkably free of junk. This time Talbot did not even try, he aimed a kick at the door and it swung wildly open into a narrow alley way.

Without ever looking back he ran as fast as he could up the alley towards the cross street at the end and ran smack into what seemed like a human wall. A very large man, the very definition in of meathead was blocking his way. Talbot staggered back and felt someone grab his arm and drag him back into the alley.

Talbot struggled for a moment and then winced as the person holding his arm twisted it, forcing Talbot to bend over almost double. He felt someone smack him hard across the face.

"Stop fuckin around, idijit!"

Talbot twisted up, trying to see who had hit him. It was a short bad man with a large belly. Next to him was the man mountain Talbot had just run into. There was at least one more person holding his arms from behind.

The balding man had a burn stick hanging from his mouth. Talbot wondered for a second what sort of mixture was in there and how dangerous the man would be if Talbot tried to run. A quick flex by the man holding him chased away that thought.

The bald man sucked in a hit of vapor and then slowly let it out. The sickly sweet smell was foreign to Talbot. The man tapped the side of his head.

"Hey. Yeah, he's here in the alley. Sure."

The man looked at Talbot, took another drag, and then aimed a swift punch into Talbot's chest. Talbot cried out but quickly stopped, screwing his eyes shut as the pain raced through him. When he opened his eyes again the man in front of him was smiling. He took another drag and this time aimed a kick at Talbot's shin. Talbot was ready and took in a sharp breath but made no sound. The man's smile faded slightly. He was sizing up where to hit next when Talbot heard a voice behind them.

"Enough, Mr. Parker!" It was Geertz, who came around next to the bald man and stared at him until Parker slinked away out of Talbot's range of vision. The man mountain remained.

"For not being protocol you sure do run like a little bitch, Mr. Talbot Singh, 121 Wright Building, Apartment 215b, which you share with your…mother and father. Nice."

Geertz's gaze shifted and Talbot could tell he was looking at a readout projected onto his cornea by an Icep, an intra-corneal electronic projection implant device. No wonder the office had been bare; he had all he needed inside his head. Talbot also knew such a device was difficult to get and very expensive: a good 10 years wage for someone like Talbot.

"So you know I'm not protocol." Talbot wheezed, his head still down, the pressure still firm on his arm.

"You are not, but it doesn't mean much. Still, no harm, no foul. And we're interested, Mr. Singh."

"Interested? About what?"

"This card, the murder of your client. Why pin this on Treasure?"

"I don't know." Talbot coughed and tasted blood. He hoped it was from the smack.

"Let him up."

Talbot felt his arm released and he slowly stood up. Geertz leaned in, his narrow face and red eyes close to Talbot.

"You will know, Mr. Singh. You work for us now, clear? Do what you need to for poor Mr. Mill, but you report back to me first what you find."

"Sure, whatever."

"Don't' fuck with me, Mr. Singh. I'm not the fucking type. Besides, go around me and there are bigger fish out there. Much bigger fish."

"Okay, alright, I get it. So, uh, my normal fee is—"

"How much is your life worth, Mr. Singh?"

"Waived. The fee is waived. Of course."

"Trust me, Mr. Singh. Trust me and things will go well for

you. Now, scurry back up to your version of safety. I'll be in touch." Geertz motioned the man mountain to move.

Talbot nodded and walked, as best he could, back down the alley to the street. He made a point of not looking back. If they were following him it would just depress him more, and if they weren't he would worry about why they weren't.

He reached the lift without incident. He figured his face was beginning to bruise. He'd have to check in at a Medrac when he got back to 29. Another expense. He was beginning to regret the entire trip.

CHAPTER THREE

By the time Talbot got back to 29 the lights had been dimmed for the evening. He walked along still bustling streets back to his apartment, only stopping to visit a Medrac unit to get the bruises on his face treated. Although the treatment cost him a good 50 credits, it got rid of most of the evidence of his run-in on 19.

His father, however, was having none of it. He grabbed his son's chin and angled it to the light over the stove.

"Your mother's in the back, reading. I don't know what happened down there and I don't want to know. Maybe she won't notice."

She did, of course. Talbot spent the next hour reassuring his mother he was okay so it was late before he could finally unfold the small couch and go to sleep in the main room. As he drifted off he thought of fantastical ways he could swing his own apartment, but none of them seemed remotely feasible.

The next morning he woke early and scuttled out of the apartment before his parents got up. He grabbed breakfast from a local cart and headed for the nearest lift to 34. The man at the gate to the lift eyed Talbot suspiciously.

"Lift goes up." He barked.

Talbot smirked and handed over the plastic card the detective had given him the day before. The man swiped it and handed it back with a surprised expression. Talbot noticed that half of the card was now black. This was really going to be a one shot deal. He briefly wondered how long he could stay there until his money ran out. Would the Treasure know to look for him up there? He guessed that if he drew on his credit account they would know.

The lift was noticeably smaller than the day before. Talbot guessed few would make the trip up, even if this lift was a local, stopping at each level. And he would bet a hot lunch few from above would bother to come down. Less traffic the further up you went.

The car was almost empty when the lift got to 34 a few minutes later. Other than him, only a woman and a small child remained. They did not get off.

Level 34 felt noticeably different to Talbot. For one thing the buildings were taller. He quickly counted eight stories. Plus the air seemed cooler, fresher even. The people seemed slightly cleaner, things slightly brighter. It was difficult for him to put a finger on any specific thing, but he knew he had gone up. Five levels made a difference, especially going up. He recalled a recent visit to level 24, where he noticed almost no difference. He recalled Olsen saying the same thing yesterday. Maybe the difference was only obvious if you went up. Did people from 24 see 29 as some sort of paradise?

He had misjudged where the protocol station was, but did not mind the extra walk. The shops seemed fuller, the people better looking. It was a pleasure to walk the streets, not a hassle. He did, however, notice fewer people. It was morning, maybe too early or maybe this level simply was less crowded. He thought probably the latter. He wondered if 29 had seemed less crowded years ago. He wondered if, in the future, people here on 34 would start subdividing their apartments and crowding more and more people into smaller and smaller spaces as the population expanded.

Protocol was located in a shiny, white building with dark blue windows. Just as all the others, the building went up to the ceiling. But the architect had cleverly foreshortened the top levels, making the building look taller, more imposing, and more powerful than its neighbors.

Talbot entered through the large glass doors on the street level and stepped into a three story atrium. He'd never seen so much open space in a building. Looking up he could see workers in their offices, the open design allowing air and light to circulate.

He looked for a bank of elevators but only saw a fairly long line of people in front of a desk. Clearly lots of people had business with the protocol this morning. Some things are no different, he mused.

To his right he noticed a small alcove where smartly dressed men and women were hurrying to. The employee entrance. With as much of a business air as he could muster, Talbot fell in behind a group of people. He was not surprised when a guard sprang up from his post in front of the alcove.

"Hold it, bud! Public entrance is over there."

Talbot briefly flashed the spent transit card, figuring it was better than nothing. "Talbot Singh to see Detective Olsen, official business." He said in a bored tone. He stood there, with an expression that said the sooner he got done whatever he was supposed to do, the better. He did not meet the guard's eyes. The guard seemed flustered for a moment then spoke into a small device on his collar.

"Olsen please. A Mr. String—"

"Singh," Talbot corrected him, stifling a yawn.

"Singh. Yes ma'am." The guard looked up, an irritated look on his face. "Any elevator, third floor."

"Thanks, man." Talbot said casually and without looking back made for the nearest elevator. He could feel the sweat run down the back of his knees.

The third floor receptionist, who barely glanced up at him, directed Talbot down the hall to a small, glassed-in office where Detective Olsen was holding the door open.

"Mr. Singh."

"Please, everyone calls me Talbot."

"Yes, well, come on in."

Talbot realized that, if anything, the detective had dressed down the day before. Her suit now was even crisper, more angular, and much more current. Her hair was up and her entire appearance suggested someone who not only wanted to look professional and stylish but could also afford to. He had to admit the effect was probably what she intended. He was thrown off a little.

"Have a seat and tell me what you found. You did find something?"

"Yes…well, sort of."

A cloud passed over Olsen's face as she watched him settle into a seat across from her desk. The office was small enough that his knees touched the front of the desk.

"Go on."

"The card is from the Treasure group. Treasure Gang, sorry."

"Okay, well, we thought as much."

"There's a problem, though."

"What?"

"I don't think it is Treasure."

"Think or know, Mr. Talbot?"

"Know. The code on the back is a year out of date—at least."

Olsen held a hand up and put a finger from her other hand to her lips. Her face, moments before cool and confident, was now worried, even a little panicked.

"I'm sorry you think so, Mr. Singh, but our lab confirmed it was a Treasure calling card," she said in a slightly too loud voice. "Sorry that you wasted time, coming here. Tell you what, there's a great fruit cart out in the plaza, let me get you something." She tilted her head towards the door.

"Uhm, sure, okay." Talbot's mind was racing. What exactly was going on? What he said clearly hit a nerve, but why?

Talbot followed Olsen out of her office and down the elevators. The detective made nervous small talk, her eyes darting as if looking for someone or something. By the time they had made it out of the building, Olsen had exhausted her small talk abilities and was quiet.

Talbot saw a cart nearby. "Can we—"

Olsen shook her head and pulled his arm away towards the street. A block later she led him into a small snack bar shop wedged next to a florist. The shop had exactly two seats. She grabbed one and motioned him to sit in the other. A tiny, elderly woman came out.

"Alda's Lemon water," Olsen said and turned to Talbot. "You?"

"Honestly, I wouldn't mind something stronger right now. Do you carry Angola beer?" The lady nodded. "Two, please." He turned back to Olsen. "Now, what the hell is going on? I'm not really into drama."

Olsen let out a long breath. "Sorry, I'm not either. Your information, is it accurate?"

"You have no idea how accurate."

"Shit…"

Talbot felt alarm rising in his stomach at seeing Olsen's composure crack.

The owner of the café brought three bottles over and set them on the table. Olsen paid with a wave of her watch and the woman nodded curtly and left. Olsen took a small sip, regained her composure, and sat up ramrod straight.

"Okay, listen, I'm not sure I know much of anything that is going on and that's what has me worried."

"Start from the beginning."

"Mr. Mill is the start. I get a call early yesterday, really early, from my super who claims he's doing a favor for someone above him. Way above. We're talking 40s, maybe higher. Wants me to handle the case personally, says that 29 protocol will clear out for me and everything."

"What the fuck?"

"I know, right? First, off they pull me down five levels for a robbery/murder set up. And they clear out the local. But, I guess if someone up there has an interest who am I to get in the way? So, I go, no problem, even after you show up."

"Thanks."

"Well, not that you aren't trouble, but I can handle locals."

"Again, thanks." Talbot drained the rest of his first bottle.

"But the more I sniffed around it was turning out to be a classic drug rebound, score settling, or something. Even when I got back analysis this morning it was almost boring. I almost bought it."

"Bought what?"

"I don't know yet, but you woke me up. Of course the card isn't right; that would be too easy."

"It's more than the card, which is why I went to the trouble, a lot of trouble, to verify it, Detective. A gang like Treasure, they're mean, vicious animals, but they're also lazy. They would never pull a hit 10 levels up, even for a money worker."

"You think Mill was a launderer?"

"He wasn't doing distro; I would have heard. Anyway, Treasure would send a local gang to do that work."

"So, the local gang leaves a Treasure card to throw off the protocol."

"No local gang can pull off that kind of stuff—or would want to. Not worth it. Treasure is pretty keen not to have people committing crime in their name. The card is pretty special. Very few groups could replicate it that well, if a little dated."

"Like who?"

Talbot arched his eyes. "Very few groups have the resources, Detective. You should know that."

"You think it's in…," Olsen stopped herself and looked down at her lap, her brow knit. "Can't be. Doesn't add up."

"Nothing about the case adds up, Detective. You said it yourself. The card is six months out of date too. It was designed to fool no one. This is why you're worried, isn't it, Detective?"

"I need to look into some stuff." Olsen stood suddenly, bumping the table and nearly upending Talbot's second beer. "Would, you be willing stay in touch? If I find anything it would help your client, I think."

Talbot drained the rest of the bottle and stood. "Tell you the truth, I think I've had enough already, Detective, but thank you."

"So right now, Mr. Mill is basically a drug dealer who's been killed by a gang. Your client's family happy with that?"

Talbot set the empty bottle down then looked at Olsen, waiting.

Olsen leaned closer. "Look, we can clear your Mr. Mill and I can make sure that whatever this is gets far, far away from me. We both win."

Talbot stood there a moment, his head slightly fuzzy from the two strong Angolans he had just sucked down.

"I'll regret this."

"Good, then."

"But…if things get to hairy I will cut and run, Detective, understood? This…," Talbot gestured at his surroundings, "is not my world, and I have no desire to make it my world. We'll get this tidied up, two days max, and then we'll go on our way."

"Of course. Alright, now, ever been to level 31?"

"A few times."

"Know the Atlanta University?"

"Sure."

"Let me tap you an address." She held out her wrist and Talbot had a flash of the jeweler on 19.

"No, here." He grabbed at his pocket, finding a small piece of paper. "Write it down. Safer."

Olsen shrugged. "Pen?"

"Shit!" Talbot turned to the counter and rang the bell. After an exchange with the owner he came back with a stubby pen.

Olsen wrote out an apartment address. "Meet me here tomorrow afternoon, say 5:00 p.m.?"

"Okay…," Talbot cocked his head wondering, Why meet at an apartment on 31?

Olsen answered his tacit question. "Long story, which I will tell you one day. Meanwhile, just wander around the level for the day. No hurry. After all, the ride down is free."

"That's the truth," Talbot muttered as Olsen turned on her heels and walked out of the tiny shop.

Talbot spent the day exploring level 34 for the rest of the day, marveling at the space—or what felt like space to him. Neat parks cropped up every few blocks, an impossibility in the overcrowded 29. He mostly stayed on the streets. Nothing in the high-priced shops interested him much. Even the food was beyond his means. He settled on a sandwich, which cost him about as much as a decent dinner for two on 29.

He left later in the afternoon feeling fairly smug. He was no climber; even this small a jump seemed like a waste to him. Despite the bigger apartments and parks, he felt no need to try and move up full-time.

On the way home he passed by Mr. Mill's shop. It was covered in black plastic. Retail space in that part of the level was always in demand and Talbot would be surprised if a new shop wasn't there by the next evening.

Talbot lay low the next day. Part of him felt like digging deeper into what Mr. Mill had been up to before his death. But part of him also knew that sniffing around might turn up something dangerous. A prickling at the back of his neck told him it was best to play dumb over the whole thing until he could figure out what was going on. Most gangs only tolerated the assists. There was an uneasy truce between gangs and assists, but it was fragile. They knew that most of the time the assists were only trying to look out for families. Assists were not protocols, and most went out of their way to avoid working with the protocol.

And yet, here he was about to meet with a detective to discuss a case that seemed to involve a gang—if not in reality, then as a fall. Talbot knew that gangs like the Treasure hated being used. And if it was someone in the protocol using them, then it would be even worse.

Talbot had half-decided to blow off meeting Olsen on 31 and forget the whole thing when the video screen he was watching flickered briefly and a small box appeared. He had a visitor. He waived his hand and the small box jumped to the main screen and revealed a slight man in a black jacket peering into the camera.

"Go away!" Talbot said.

"Mr. Singh, I bring greeting from a Mr. Geertz." Talbot sat upright, panicked. "It's a good thing, Mr. Singh, not a bad thing," the man assured him, looking over his shoulder a few times.

Talbot rolled his eyes and punched in the access code. He

only had a few moments so he grabbed the only weapon he knew he could carry: a long stick he'd sharpened. If he was out on the street, anything else would be picked up. He just hoped that whoever was coming up did not have a way to smuggle something more effective than a sharp stick.

There was a soft buzz. Talbot moved to the door. He could see two people on the screen.

Fuck.

He let them in and recognized at once the tall, thin figure of Mr. Geertz. Talbot said nothing as the shorter, stockier man looked around and let out a low whistle.

"Nice fuckin palace, bud. You get this from reward money from the protocol?"

"My parents' place," Talbot growled.

"Quiet, Jenson! Of course it isn't protocol cash. Mind if we sit, Mr. Singh?"

"Yes," Talbot muttered as Geertz settled on the couch.

"I'll be brief, Mr. Singh. I've got business elsewhere. Sit, sit. Surely you did not think I came all the way up here just for you? No, but you are still of some importance. Tell me, how did your trip up to 34 go? Meet some interesting people?"

"Maybe." Talbot tried not to register surprise. Of course Geertz knew.

Geertz waived his long, bony hand airily. "Time is money, Mr. Singh. And let's be completely honest here, your life is worth very little money."

"One person. You know who."

"Olsen, yes. Charming lady, no?"

"Not especially," Singh said.

"She is…complex. What did she tell you?"

"I told her. I told her about the card. Her protocol told her it was Treasure. I assured her it wasn't."

"Good, good. So, what happens next?"

"Nothing. It's a screwy. I'm done. She knows it wasn't Treasure, so I'm done."

Silence hung in the air. Geertz stared impassively at Talbot. "Well, then," He stood up, took a step forward, and then stopped to look down at the still seated Talbot. "If, for any reason, this detective wants to pursue the case, it would be most helpful if you went along with her, just to keep tabs on her actions. It would be well worth your time, and mine, Mr. Singh. Consider this, will you?"

"I'll keep an open mind," Talbot said, staring at the rug, sweat forming at the back of his neck.

"Excellent!"

Geertz and the stocky man left and closed the door behind them without saying another word. Talbot let out a ragged breath; he had not realized he had stopped breathing. He stood up and grabbed a jacket. He guessed he was going to level 31 after all.

CHAPTER FOUR

The ride up wasn't too bad, but Talbot made a mental note to say something to Olsen about how often they could meet. A few trips up and he would have to dip into savings. He wasn't going to make any money on the Mill case; he'd already spent most of his advance fee.

The apartment address that Olsen had given him was in an older district, near one of the city's better universities, Atlanta. Most of the good universities were located on 31 or higher. Lower than that and you were stuck with mostly technical institutes. Talbot knew lots of people who had gone to them on 29 and learned trades. In his mind only the vague and pretentious would have applied to universities on 31. It was a sure sign of a climber to send your kids to Atlanta. It assured them better jobs and, if they did well and made the right connections, assured them a place on a higher level.

But why someone from 34 would want to meet here was bothering Talbot. Maybe it was a friend, a place away from 34 where Olsen felt safe. He rang the bell and was buzzed in.

The building felt old, solid. It was unlike any building he'd been in on 29. Despite the fact that he knew level 31 was built after

29, it just felt older. He knew that much of 29 had been periodically leveled to make room for new, more compact and room-efficient buildings. Maybe this building, Olsen's, really was older than anything on 29 by virtue of being left to stand since it was built.

Inside the building was cool, clean, minimal, and yet clearly, effortlessly elegant. The lift in the foyer was twice as large as the one in Talbot's apartment. He idly fingered the brass railing as it raced upwards six short stories. The doors opened silently and he stepped into a wide, carpeted hallway. It was free of the storage units and mech boxes that Talbot was so used to seeing in hallways on 29. He marveled at how nice the place was and wondered what Olsen's apartment on 34 was like. He checked himself, shaking his head at the idea of being in that woman's apartment. The he laughed at himself for being such a sad case: he was more interested in the woman's apartment than in her.

As he reached to press the apartment buzzer, the door swung open and Olsen smiled from behind it.

"Come on in."

Talbot took in the apartment. He eyes lingered over the space. It was cavernous. He estimated the main room was easily 15 feet wide and 20 feet deep. A series of odd video screens lined the far wall, tasteful and subdued art decorated the rest. There were low-lying shelves filled with what he knew to be books. The smell was musty but not unpleasant. To his right as he came in was a small kitchenette with a sit-in bar separating it from the main room.

"Nice," he murmured, more to himself.

"Thanks. And thanks for coming up."

"This yours?" he asked, approaching one of the shelves to

look more closely at the bound paper volumes on it.

"Yeah…well, sort of."

"Love nest?" He regretted it as soon as he said it. "I mean, not that."

"No, nothing like that." she said, her tone cooler. "This was my father's flat."

The implication of what she'd said took a moment to register with Talbot. The realization must have shown on his face. Olsen laughed lightly.

"Yeah, I'm one of those: lifters. Climbers, you called them?"

"So, you grew up."

"I grew up here, sure. Daddy was a professor at the University. So, naturally, he wanted the best for me, best school, best opportunities, best life. I went to a university on 33, got a job a level up…every girl's dream."

"Everyone's dream," Talbot repeated, staring at Olsen as if trying to figure her out all again. Complex was what Geertz had said.

"Well, not everyone I guess. You seem pretty happy on 29. Not that there's anything wrong."

"It's okay. Home is where you make it." He turned his attention back to the books.

"That's just it though, Talbot; you've got to make it your home. Don't you ever want something more? Look at this place: it's nice, sure, even for here. But compare this to 29 and the kind of place you could afford there. I've seen them; they're so cramped."

Talbot looked up. "You've been in one? I thought that—"

"Mill's," she said quickly, turning back to the kitchen and

took two glasses out of a cabinet and grabbed a bottle out of the fridge. "But seriously, you're pretty sharp, certainly capable. You should ride up, as they say."

"No one says that."

"They do on 34," she smiled and handed him a glass. "Sythine, better than average breed."

Talbot eyed it suspiciously. "How do you know I drink?"

"You guzzled two beers yesterday, not exactly grueling detective work. If you're a practicing devotee, you're pretty bad at it," she smiled at her joke.

Talbot took a sip and wondered how many glasses she had prior to his arrival. The drink was sweet, slightly nutty—better than the stuff he could afford on 29. "So, what did you find out about Mr. Mill?"

Olsen sighed and plopped into an overstuffed chair. "You're changing the topic. Why are you stuck on 29, Talbot?"

"Who says I'm stuck? I like it there. What can I tell you?"

"Okay, but don't you ever feel stifled there? Don't you ever think about all of those levels up above us and what they're like?"

"Sure, sometimes. Who doesn't? I watch the telenovelas too."

"They're all fake, you know."

Talbot cocked his head.

"They're fake, not real. All those people living their lives on level 60 or whatever? Filmed on 43."

"Okay."

"So, even if you watch those things you have no idea...," Olsen's voice trailed off. Her body language suggested a renewed clarity. "Mr. Mill, yes." She flicked her wrist and a projection popped up. "Very…unimpressive, which might be curious in itself. Third-rate jeweler, sold mostly crap. Did well enough, though. Kids all went to either tech or university. Never got into any real trouble. Couple of customer complaints but was able to smooth them over, even if they went to House Control."

"I could have told you all of that."

"Sure. Now, tell me what the folks in Infotel did not Talbot."

"Born and bred in 29, married a climber from 28. No big deal. Daughter went to tech on 28 for mech work; she has a daughter that should be tech or uni herself. Two other kids, sons. One works across the level, an organizer for a food chain. The other son died."

"Died how?"

"Well, it's the only thread, really." Talbot said, slowly, relishing the small drama he could reveal. "He got into a gang, something went wrong. Always does."

"Treasure?"

"No," Talbot sighed. "Treasure doesn't operate that way. It was a 29 gang not aligned with Treasure. And, and, and—before you ask—it wasn't some sort of retaliation thing. He crossed his own gang. And it was years ago."

"How long?"

"Ten, 11."

"Still, interesting connection. Even if just random. Mill had knowledge of the gangs, of the system."

"He was a jeweler. He probably paid protection to at least one, if not more. Really, Detective."

"Aria"

"What?"

"My name is Aria. Sorry if my lack of knowledge of the butter gets you down, Talbot."

Talbot laughed. "Well, now that I know you come from 31 I think you may know more than most on 34. Anyway, sorry. You should be happy that gangs are a little less influential on 34."

"I am. But back to Mill, now that there is a connection."

"No, no connection," he insisted, "just…randomness. Look, ask 10 people on 29 about gangs and nine will know someone in one or have dealt with one. It's a slender thread and if you pull it, it will just break. Dead end."

"Okay, so what else?"

"Not much. He was a crappy jeweler. That much you got right."

"Maybe a disgruntled customer. Would someone from Treasure, or some random gang, get mad at him for selling them crap?"

"Sure, but that would be stupid on all accounts. Mill would never sell someone like that junk and most people like that—especially if it happened to be some random Treasure guy coming up for air—would have known to steer clear of some junk dealer like Mill."

"More synthine?" Aria asked, pouring herself another glass. Talbot waived her off.

"So tell me about yourself, Talbot. You know all about me and my sordid lifter past."

"Hmm, I'm pretty sure I don't know half your story. So, been working as an assist since I was 16 or so. On my own since I was 19."

"Is there a Mrs. Singh—or mister?"

Talbot laughed. "No, none of the above. Between girlfriends, as they say."

"Really? Shocked. You seem pretty sturdy, likable, if a little stuck up."

"I'm stuck up? How much did that suit cost you?" Talbot laughed again. "Nah, I just seem to come across as…not boyfriend material. I still live at home."

Aria waved her hand. "That I do know about 29—space is at a premium. Another reason to move up. Maybe—just going out on a limb here—maybe your lack of ambition is what's turning off the girls, not the parents."

"I don't have time for climbers."

Aria stood up, her head high. "Screw you and your lifter issues, Talbot. It's boring. You're trapped down there. You're smart, not bad looking, and you also know you're trapped. One day you'll wake up old, alone, trapped in a sea of low-level immis…all of who are going to be elbowing you on their way up. "

She knelt down beside him as he turned away. "Don't waste it, Talbot."

"You've had enough." Talbot tried to grab her glass but she quickly sloshed back the remaining synthine. "Never. We all want more kiddo."

"Not everyone."

"Everyone. We'd be stuck in the bottom of a swamp, laying in the mud if we didn't want more." She sat back, resting with her legs tucked behind her. "It's not wrong to want more." Talbot was surprised to see Aria's eyes were moist. "It's not wrong, is it? People know. They look at you. They know, but it's not wrong," she whispered, her eyes now full of tears. Talbot slid off the couch and knelt in front of her, trying to gently lift her by the arm. She resisted.

"I think maybe you should rest, Aria."

"I know what you think, Talbot. I know you think I'm just some sort of scummy jump girl, wanting more and more. But I don't. I just want what I earn, what I deserve. There's nothing wrong with that."

"No, I guess not," he said evenly.

"Then why do you look at me like that? Why do you hate my ambition?"

"I don't."

"You do. Crabs in a fucking pot is all."

"Aria, look, I know I sound…I think we got off on the wrong foot. You didn't exactly welcome me."

"You weren't supposed to be there, Talbot. It was closed; that was the mistake."

"I know, but…I know. Sorry."

"No, it's okay, I'm beginning to see why you were there. You're good at what you do—dogged, determined. You could do so…can I kiss you?"

Talbot sat back.

"Sorry, sorry, that was the Sythine," Aria mumbled. "I bet you think I'm a pretty cold one."

"No, but you do throw off a certain vibe."

"Kiss me, Talbot. I can show you." She leaned in and touched Talbot's lips with hers. She did feel warm. Talbot felt something snap inside. Something that had been pent up. He knew in that instant that it had less to do with Aria than with where he was in his life. He did not resist the kiss and responded back.

Talbot woke up in a slight panic before remembering where he was. Aria was asleep beside him in the bed. He carefully slid the sheet off and quietly got up. The room was dim, the shades drawn, keeping most of the artificial day out. He padded into the bathroom. The light flickered on as he washed his face. He took a long look at the reflection staring back at him. He was nearly 30, not especially fit but not overweight. No grey hairs yet. A neat beard trimmed along the jaw. As he stared his eyes slid and his face melted into an indistinct blur.

He could not deny the previous few hours hadn't been good, fun almost. It had been nice to hold another person so close and to be intimate with them. He had missed that. But he knew what happened had been the beginning and the end all at once. He knew he should want more of it. And he did, but not with Aria.

When he went back to the bedroom to get pants Aria was sitting up. She had a small glass of water and was swallowing several pills.

"Mmmm. Off so soon?"

"I was going to let you sleep. Thought you might need it."

"Not with these," she held up a small vial. "I should be good as new in a few minutes."

Talbot shrugged into a shirt. "I think you should drop the Mill case."

"That your way of telling me this was a one night stand?"

"No, but yeah, it was a one night stand, Aria, I think we both know that."

"It doesn't have to be, Talbot. We're not bad together, we had fun. Like I said, you've got talent—as an assist too," she laughed and drank the rest of the water. "I could get you a place in protocol or with one of the private agencies on 34—"

"No."

"Okay, okay. Why close up Mill?"

"Just…nothing there. We both know that."

"I'm not sure. But you seem keen on shutting it down." She stood up, naked. Despite himself, Talbot blushed. She smiled and reached for the robe hanging on the bathroom door. "What aren't you telling me?"

"Nothing, just…look, we've both got better things to do. You don't need to hang around 29 and I don't need to spend any more time or money on the case. If you leave the case his family will be happy. I will smooth things over with them, and I'll get some money out of this and…we're done." He made the motion of washing his hands.

Aria eyed Talbot, tilting her head.

"So this is the kiss off then?"

"If you say so."

"No, Talbot, you're saying so. Fine, alright, consider it closed. I can file a report of no findings, which isn't exactly a lie." She pulled her long black hair back and tied it at her neck. "My offer still stands, if you want to come on up."

"Yeah, well, thanks all the same."

"Just remember, Talbot, not a crime to be ambitious."

CHAPTER FIVE

Talbot took the lift down to 29, willing his mind blank the entire way. He felt it best not to think too much about it. After letting himself into his parents' apartment, he sent a message to Mill's widow, telling her the case had been closed. He then got out his sleep bag and crashed on the couch until his parents got home from work that evening.

Talbot spent the next few days in a fog. He settled the Mill account, partially replenishing his savings with the fee. He'd barely broke even after factoring in the many elevators trips he had taken. At the end of the week he joined some friends to celebrate his 30th birthday. As he sat there in the crowded club, the sound of drums ringing in his ears, he thought about what Aria had said. Forget it, he kept telling himself. But he could not forget it.

Several hours later as he made his way inside his apartment building, a small, grey-haired woman accosted him. "Singh! Where you been?"

"Mama Mill," Talbot said, faking happiness. "I've been out with friends. Thank you for settling on the case. Sorry about Mr. Mill."

"To hell with that; the old man had it coming. Bigger problem now, Singh, and you gotta fix it fast! Jessica's daughter Jahn is missing. Gone!"

"Your granddaughter?"

"Same. Whatever you need, do it and fast. You got connections. You get her back, right?"

Talbot shook his head to clear it. "Uh, yes, of course. Where was she?"

"At the uni on 31. Atlanta."

"Wait, what? Atlanta?"

"Yes! You drunk, Singh? Better get the sober and quick."

"Yes, sure. We'll get her back."

"You'd better. No pay for you this time unless you get her back in one piece, Mister," the old lady poked a finger at his chest.

"Yes, of course I will."

Talbot did not go up but instead turned around and went to the nearest Medrac down the street. A shot later his head felt much clearer, his pockets lighter. He then went back to his building and knocked on the apartment door where Mrs. Mill lived.

She opened the door and wordlessly let him in. It was almost a duplicate of his parent's apartment. Inside the cramped space, sitting on an old couch, was a thin woman with long black hair. Her eyes were red.

"You remember Jessica?" Mrs. Mill nodded towards her daughter.

Talbot nodded. He sat down next to Jessica. It was the only open seat in the tiny room. "It's been a while. Your Mom says that your daughter is missing."

Jessica looked up from her lap, eyes full of tears. Talbot

remembered her as a stunning beauty years ago, an older family friend that had fueled his imagination. Now he almost felt embarrassed about those childhood thoughts. The woman sitting beside him was still striking but her face was lined, her skin blotchy. Jessica took a deep breath and let it out ragged.

"When did she go missing?" Talbot asked in a low, calm tone.

"It's…it's been two days. She went out with friends, for drinks I guess. Who knows? But she went to the bathroom and never came back."

"So her friends noticed her missing then?"

"Yes, after a few minutes, when she didn't come back. They looked everywhere in the club."

"And no word so far?"

"Word?"

"Demands for ransom, that kind of thing."

"No," she shook her head and launched into a new round of sobbing.

Talbot turned towards Mama Mill. "Her father?"

"He's gone, long time ago. Never hear from him. Dead probably," she replied.

"Why do you think he is dead?"

"Low-life scum, mixed up in lots of nonsense."

"Any help from the uni?"

"Not a peep. I reported to them myself, but all they say is that they'll monitor her accounts. Said it was off-campus—not under their control, not their problem. Lousy shits."

"How long was Jahn at Atlanta?" he asked Jessica.

"Two years."

"Scholarship?"

"Sh-she was there on a full one, biotech. Straight As." came the muffled voice of Jessica.

Talbot got up and motioned Mrs. Mill into the relative privacy of the kitchenette. He kept his voice low, although he was sure that Jessica could still hear every word. "I'll need to go up to 31 to talk to her friends. Tap me their info or have Jessica. If you hear any word, especially ransom demands, call me right away."

Mama Mill nodded.

"I'll do everything I can to find her Jessica. I have some connections. I'll try my best." His mind wandered to Aria. Probably not the string he wanted to pull, even if there was a connection to the recently deceased Mr. Mill. His mind clicked for a moment.

"Was Jahn close to your husband?"

"Yes, she was his favorite. He was so proud. They used to walk around town, looking through junk stores, talking."

"What about?"

"Everything. I asked him once why he liked going to the stores. One can't be too careful, although I know my husband was nothing but proper with his granddaughter."

"Of course."

"I asked her about, you know, and she laughed and laughed. She said they just talked—about everything."

Talbot's neck felt tingly as he repeated, "Everything..."

Talbot all but ran down to the street, taking the stairway

when the elevator wouldn't come fast enough. He had told Mrs. Mill he was going to 31, but he now realized he had to get to 34 first. It would almost drain him but he had to do it. He checked his watch: it was 2:00 a.m. He reluctantly headed back to his parent's flat to wait out the night.

He did not sleep at all, his mind a wired whirl. At 6:00 a.m. he took a shower and when he came out of the bathroom he found his mother in the kitchenette sliding breakfast onto a plate.

"How was your birthday, Tal?" she asked brightly.

He grunted. "Been up all night. Got a new job."

"A new one?" she asked, a note of concern in her voice.

"Mrs. Mill's granddaughter's gone missing at the uni."

"No! And on top of her husband."

"'Fraid so. I'm off to 31 to talk to her friends."

His mother looked up from her plate, eyes narrow.

"Talbot, you can no more lie than I can fly. Is there a connection with Mr. Mill's death and this girl?"

"Maybe, Mom. Look, no time. I do have to go up and I want to be there early. I'll phone later."

"Promise?"

"Yes, no worries. Just lots of talking today. I swear."

She sighed. "I just worry, you know. You are all we have, your father and I."

"I know, Mom, I know."

"So at least tell me what is going on?"

"Well, she was close to Mr. Mill. The protocol seem to think that Mr. Mill was mixed up in gangs."

"Never!"

"Seems strange. He would cheat you five ways from noon, but I don't think he was that bad. Anyway, if he told anyone about what he was doing it would be his granddaughter. His own daughters were grown, living outside the home."

"So you think a gang snatched her?"

"No telling. I just need to talk to some folks at Atlanta. Just a word I promise, nothing more."

"Words always get you into trouble, Tal. Be careful."

"Everything gets me into trouble," he muttered as he opened the front door.

"I heard that!"

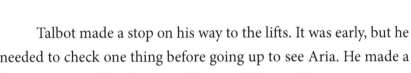

Talbot made a stop on his way to the lifts. It was early, but he needed to check one thing before going up to see Aria. He made a detour to a small bar down a side street. Next to the entrance was a call box. Talbot chuckled to himself. The Treasure may have known where he lived, but he knew where Geertz's henchman Jenson lived too. He had recognized the squirrelly man when he and Geertz had come up to Talbot's apartment. Jenson was a low-level pusher of various products. Talbot made it part of his business to know where people like him hung out.

Talbot pushed the button. The screen remained blank, so he pushed again. It remained stubbornly blank for a few minutes while Talbot held his finger on the button. It flickered to life and a blearily-eyed Jenson sidled onto the screen.

"Stay there, fucker. I'm gonna blast your ass in about five

seconds."

"I need to talk to our friend," Talbot said.

Jenson's eyes opened a fraction more. "Better be good, little drip. If I had my way I'd a put you down long ago."

The door buzzed and Talbot pushed his way inside. He took the stairs to Jenson's apartment, not wanting the disadvantage of coming out of an elevator's confined space. He entered the hallway without incident and knocked on the door. It swung open and Talbot looked inside. The place was tiny, even by 29 standards. Barely a few feet wide and, Talbot guessed, probably 10 feet long. It was one room with a bed and a fold-away kitchen. Jenson sat on the bed, pulling on a shirt. The air was stale and infused with some sort of synthetic chemical Talbot could not put his finger on.

Jenson stood up and put a stubby finger in Talbot's face. "This better be good. Rule was, we contacted you. You got nerve draggin' your proto-ass-kissing self here."

Talbot ignored the finger and scowled. "You able to get Geertz on a line, secure? I know it's early."

"He don't sleep."

"Can you do it then?"

Jenson growled but said nothing. He reached over and pulled out a small, flat dull metal box. He beat a short tattoo on the top making it glow green and a few seconds later a voice rose out of the box.

"Mr. Geert. That ass Talbot is here."

"We don't know anything about the girl, Mr. Singh."

Talbot laughed in spite of himself, Jenson shot him a dirty look. "Sorry, but you don't know anything? I haven't even said hello and you have a ready answer for the reason I came? I think you know plenty."

"No, Mr. Singh, we don't. We know that she was taken."

"How?"

"The uni reported it to protocol. Naturally we have some tethers on people connected to Mr. Mill."

"So you no idea what might have happened?"

"Traffickers perhaps, Mr. Singh, but not Treasure or our relations. But that is not why you are here, is it?"

"No, I needed…I wanted to make sure I didn't step."

"Are you headed back to 34 then? Get Detective Olsen to reopen the Mill case, think there is a connection?"

"Yeah, well…"

"Careful, Mr. Singh. Don't get involved with a woman like Olsen. I guess that since you met her at her 31 love nest you know she's not all she seems."

"How…okay, what else do you know about her?"

There was a moment silence. "What do you want to know, Singh? I can tell you what she buys at the hypermart, what holos she goes to."

"Can I trust her if I go back and get her help on the girl?"

"Can you trust anyone? She's a lifter, Singh, difficult to keep track of. I don't know if she will help you or not. I suspect that whatever fling she had with you was based on her primal needs and not material. You showing up might not play into her long-term plans."

"Who said anything about a fling?"

"Please, Mr. Singh."

"Okay." Talbot closed his eyes for a moment to block out the grinning and leering Jenson. "So I can push ahead then?"

"Yes, the girl was Mill's granddaughter. There may be a connection."

"Yes, I was thinking that," Talbot said, glad to steer the conversation away from his love life.

"My guess is traffickers, but none we have connections with. I will tell you if I hear anything."

"How do I get in touch?"

"Jenson will find you."

Talbot rolled his eyes as Jenson pointed his finger at him. The box stopped glowing and the room was silent. Talbot turned around and left without looking back.

CHAPTER SIX

On his way to the station the lights above changed from night mode to day mode. Except for a few early morning walkers the streets were mostly empty. The lift station was deserted. He figured his best course of action was to go to 34 first, track down Aria, and then on the way back stop off at 31. This would also be the cheapest route since it was free to go down.

He winced as he downloaded enough credits onto his transit app from his bank account. Settling into a seat at the rear of the lift, a habit he had learned from his mentor, Talbot wondered how Aria would take his quick reappearance. He'd thought about calling ahead, but remembered Geertz's advice. It unnerved him how much Treasure knew about his movements.

When the lift arrived at 34 people were beginning to fill the streets. It struck Talbot somewhat strange how all the levels still conditioned people to the natural daylight cycle, albeit one based on the needs of business rather than the populace. Day lights came on at 6:00 a.m. and went off at 9:00 p.m., but it was never truly dark on any level. Talbot idly wondered for a moment what it must be like to be under a real night sky.

Rather than try to get up into Aria's office, Talbot staked out a position in the small plaza in front of the building. He waited for almost an hour before spotting her moving in a crowd that had spilled out of the tube station next to the building. He fell into step next to her.

"Hey, fancy a cup of something?" he asked in a low voice.

Her reaction was visceral. She shook as if electricity was flowing through her. "Talbot, what on earth on you doing here?"

"Been a development. Seriously, we need to grab some coffee and talk. Know of a place that serves food too? I'm starving."

She stopped, a smile forming on her face. "Tal, look, what we did was fun, but…"

"It's not about that. Mill's granddaughter's been snatched."

A strange expression flashed on Aria's face, Talbot wasn't sure if it is was fear or exasperation. She recovered quickly. "Shit. You think it is connected?"

"Yes, but not here."

"Yeah, okay. Follow me."

Aria took Talbot by the hand and dragged him against the oncoming crowd into a small café in the building next door to the protocol station. This one was much larger than the last one they had ducked into. It had a large section of tables off to the side. After getting coffee and a roll for Talbot they settled at a table away from the main part of the café.

"What happened?" Aria asked. She leaned back, arms folded across her chest.

"Mill's Granddaughter was snatched from the uni on 31, Atlanta. She's a student there."

"For fuck's sake."

"It gets worse. According to Mrs. Mill, her husband treated the girl like a daughter. They hung out together, he spoiled her, and they talked. A lot."

Aria understood where he was going. "So she might know what Mill was up to."

"Maybe, maybe not. But maybe whoever snatched her thinks she did."

"Okay, but that's fairly thin. People disappear all the time, how do you she was even snatched?"

"Her family knows."

Aria said nothing and studied her coffee.

"Aria, I know there is a connection here. It's too much of a coincidence."

"Maybe. Probably. But what can I do? It's a missing person for 31."

"Reopen Mill. Connect some dots. I'm sure protocol on 31 will cooperate."

"You sure, are you?" she smiled. "I'm not."

"I just need some help, is all. So don't open the case; just let me know if you hear or see anything."

"Have you been to the uni yet? Talked to anyone?"

"No, not yet. I came here first."

"Good. Okay, I can help as long as you keep it down low. If anyone here finds out or if the people on 31 find out you have help from 34…"

"Really? Is it that bad?"

"What? You want to find out? Go ahead, but you can't undo

stuff. If you want to find this girl we need to make sure no one gets their panties in a twist."

"Okay, okay. So what's next? I go down to Atlanta and find out what they know?"

"Yeah. We can meet tonight at the place on 31. I can be there by 6:00 p.m. I'll do as much digging around here as I can. "

Talbot gave her all the info he had on the girl. They both got up from the table.

"Tal, sorry about the way I reacted. I thought maybe you'd, you know, come back..."

"It's okay. I understand."

"I don't think you do. Ever since that afternoon, I—"

"Aria, there's no need to explain. It was fun, but you made it pretty clear that I'm not your type, lacking the ambition and all."

Aria looked momentarily hurt. "And am I your type? I'm not going to settle down on 29 and raise kids."

"I never—"

"You don't have to, Tal. Look, sorry. This is the real reason I regretted that afternoon, no other reason. This arguing is making us nuts."

"No, you're right. I 'm sorry too. Let's just be cool about it, alright?"

"Sure," Aria said, but her voice was full of doubt.

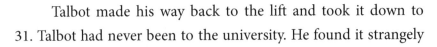

Talbot made his way back to the lift and took it down to 31. Talbot had never been to the university. He found it strangely separated from the rest of the level. A row of unified buildings lined the main street in front of the campus, presenting a stern, grey wall with black windows that appeared to go on for at least four blocks long. However, once you went through the sole entrance, you entered a large area that was about a block square that was open to the ceiling seven stories above. Arranged in a neat little pattern were small one story buildings, and between them were trees, actual trees, that, as far as Talbot could tell, were alive.

Talbot walked over to the nearest one and, scanning quickly to make sure no one was looking, reached out and touched the bark. He had seen trees before, usually in the distance, in parks where you had to pay to get into, or in hotel lobbies on upper levels, but had never actually been able to touch one. The bark felt very different from anything he had ever felt before. Most things in his life were synthetic. He left his hand on the bumpy, slightly warm surface for several moments.

He had spent 30 years in the city, he had never been outside of it. No one he knew had ever been outside of it. He wasn't even sure how, if one wanted, to get outside. He resolved to find out; maybe Aria knew of a way.

He must have looked pretty strange standing there, his palm resting on a tree trunk. A security guard made his way over to Talbot, coughing lightly as he approached. Startled, Talbot quickly withdrew his hand.

"Can I help you?"

Talbot tried his best smile. "Uh, yeah, actually. I need to talk to someone in security. In the offices I mean, about a student."

"Across the quad, go behind that green building on the left to the building marked #34. The office is on the entrance floor."

"Thanks." Talbot hurried off across the open square, eager to put distance between himself and the guard. He felt foolish for getting caught practically fondling the tree. The guard probably took him for some lower level yokel. Talbot's face flushed at the thought.

The security office was tucked in the back of a large white building with a low overhanging front and long narrow windows that went from the ground to the ceiling above. Inside the office was a small reception area staffed by a bored young man, who appeared to be a student in the uni or recent grad. Talbot explained why he was there and tapped a card from his watch to the reception computer. The guy behind the desk did not even look at it. He lazily stabbed the air, called out Erica!, and told Talbot have a seat.

One uncomfortable minute later a large, beefy woman came into the room. She wore the same dull grey uniform as the security man by the tree. She looked tired, harried. Talbot had a sinking feeling this would not go well.

"You Singh? Saw your card. Assist, eh? This about the Stovall girl?"

"Yes, Jahn Sotvall."

The woman deflated a little. "Figured you'd show up. Erica Gleeson, shift manager."

"Nice to meet you. Can you help me or do I need to see a director?"

"Director's out sick. She won't be back until tomorrow soonest. You could wait until the deputy director gets in this afternoon, but he'll give you the same report I will."

"Which is?"

"Nothin'. Look, it's not personal. It's just uni policy. We gave the protocol a report."

"Which I haven't seen."

"That's gonna be your problem then, right? I can't give that out to anyone, even the family assist."

"Then don't. Just let me look it over."

Gleeson looked back at him blankly. She sighed and motioned him to come with her. He followed her through a door into a back area. They went down a warren of small cubbies until they got to one that was totally bare of any decorations. It just had a floating screen in one corner. Gleeson made a gesture and the screen flickered. A moment later a small paragraph of print was floating. Talbot quickly read through it.

"That's it?"

"That's the protocol report."

"There's nothing else you can tell me? There's nothing there, just her name, the date, times. I mean, have you spoken to anyone? Her friends?"

"That's all on the protocol. Listen, Singh, let me tell you: students go missing all the time here. We have 43,000 students registered, give or take. They go on benders, they run back home, they get married, or dive down several levels to live the real life. She's been gone for what, three days?"

"So you think she ran off to get married? Really?"

"Or dropped some levels."

"She's from 29. She doesn't need to get real; she came from real." Talbot spat out the last couple of words.

Gleeson swiped the screen closed and then stood back, her arms folded. She was silent.

"Can I speak to her friends, roommates?"

"If you got their numbers they can chat with you all day long, it's a free state," Gleeson said, her tone now frosty.

"Great, thanks then. I'll just see myself out." Talbot turned and left the office without looking back.

Talbot wanted nothing more than to go out into the large open square again and look at the trees, but as he entered the area he saw at least two security guards looking directly at him. He figured it was best to leave and regroup.

As he exited the large buildings that surrounded the square and went back into the world of level 31, he felt a weight descend on him for the first time that he could remember. The ceiling, seven stories above, seemed closer and more oppressive than before. The air smelled stale and the streets seemed somehow dirty. He noticed a thin layer of dust over everything.

After walking several blocks he found a small park with benches and some sad potted flowers. No trees. He sat down and pulled up his watch.

"Mrs. Mill?"

"Singh! What have you found, boy?"

"Not much. Security on campus is not being very helpful. I was wondering if you had contact information for any of Janh's friends."

"Hmm, her mother may. I'll tell her to send them to you. If not, what are you going to do, Singh?"

"Not sure, Momma Mill. I got some people working on it."

"You talk to the gangs, boy?"

"Yes, some. They have no idea, and yes I can trust them. Trouble is I'm not as sure who is working on 31 or at the uni. Mrs. Mill, what club was Jahn at that night?"

"I got it right here…wait… Ecstasy 586. You know it?"

"No, but it's coming up as listed. I'll head there, see if they're open. I'll look for those contacts, okay?"

Talbot hung up. The club was only a few blocks from campus. No surprise. The edges of the large uni were filled with bars, clubs, and snack palaces. Talbot found the club easily. It had a large, gaudy gold and pink neon sign out front that was on even under day lights. There were no hours listed but the front door swung open easily and Talbot went inside.

The club seemed unremarkable on first glance. The lights were brighter than they would be at night and the depressing litter of plastic chairs and wobbly tables scattered around the large open room lent it more the air of a sad mental ward than a night club. The stage, decked out in gaudy silver spangles, offered further evidence this was not one of the top flight clubs. Maybe at night, under lights and with loud music, it felt more special. Talbot doubted it.

A heavyset, tall man came through double doors in the back, tugging a large sled loaded with boxes. "Closed!" he shouted. "Come back at five."

Talbot tapped his watch and flashed a large screen with his name and ID info. "Talbot Singh, assist working with the Mill family. I wanted to talk to someone who was working here the night Jahn Stovall disappeared."

The man brought the sled up to where Talbot was standing

and grimaced. "I was head of bar that night. I already told protocol: don't know nothin'"

Talbot looked around the room. "How many bar folks you got working in a place like this?"

The man screwed up his eyes in thought. "That was a Friday? We had 14, including a couple of bar-back runners. Plus the bouncers and DJs."

"Waiters?"

"No waiters. Bar service only."

"So you remember the night?"

"Well, yeah. Never happened before since I been here. Business has been off a little since. Like I said, none of us saw nothin'. We already went over this with protocol."

"Well they somehow omitted that from their report."

The large man snorted. "You could fill 10 chips with what they leave out of stuff. Every time there's a fight."

"You got gangs here?"

The man stopped short, his face going stony. "In this club, never. Won't put up with 'em."

Talbot held up his hand. "Stop. I'm not the protocol, okay? I've dealt with enough places like this. Just tell me what gangs work in here."

The man opened his mouth to protest then shook his head slightly. "Mostly Skills. They're local, minor stuff. You want something, they got it."

"So mostly drugs?"

"Yeah. Seriously, we don't put up with anything else. You want flesh you gotta go someplace else."

"The Skills, they maintain here?"

"Yeah, pretty well. Sometimes we get tussles when other gangs come in, but the bouncers keep it pretty clean."

"Any Treasure up in here ever?"

"Nah, we're not that big time. The kind of stuff they push our kids couldn't afford. Look, Mister, these kids want beer, synthine, maybe some numb killers or pushers, but there's not much else in here."

"And people who go missing?"

"Been here three years, never heard of anyone else than that girl. Before me, who knows? But the owner said he'd never had anyone go missing from here. This ain't a pick out joint. You go over a street, some places there you take the wrong drug, talk to the wrong people, you find yourself 10 levels down when you wake up. Happens about three, four times a year."

"They trafficked?"

He shook his head, "Nah. Kidnapped, ransom, transport fare back up at double or triple the rates. Look, it's not legal, but it's pretty small time around here, even when it's bad. And not in here," he added, with a little too much emphasis for Talbot's liking.

He felt a small buzz on his wrist. He glanced at his watch and saw contact info flowing in from Jahn's mother.

"Thanks. Look, if you hear anything contact me, okay?"

"I don't work with protocol, bud."

"I'm the family's assist." He saw a confused look on the bartender's face. "The polish? Look, all I want is the girl back, no questions asked."

"Sure, pal." Talbot grabbed a small projection that sprung

from his watch and flicked it over to the bartender. It vanished into the man's own wrist.

When Talbot got outside he pulled up watch screen to look at the information he'd received. The three women Jahn had been with that night. He saw that two of them lived together outside the uni, but the third was in a dorm. That might be more difficult. He could call her and ask to meet outside, but he wanted to keep as much of the communication offline as he could. Already he realized that Geertz would have picked up that he now knew about the three friends.

As he crossed the street and headed to the two women's apartment his watch buzzed again. It was an anonymous message, but he knew who it was right away. Apartment 6:00 p.m. He sighed. Anonymous messages were pretty expensive; he had almost never gotten any. He was pretty sure Geertz could trace that one too without knowing who sent it. He'd have to talk to Aria about that when they met.

CHAPTER SEVEN

The apartment belonging to the two women was about five blocks away. The further away he got from the uni the less seedy and less cluttered with bars and snack palaces the streets became. Talbot checked his watch. It was noon. Lunchtime. He was taking a chance the two would even be home and not in class or on the campus for other reasons.

They lived in a large, sprawling block of flats. Their tidy but cheap appearance gave away their true function: uni housing. Great, Talbot thought. He was going to have to tread carefully. He buzzed their callbox. A small screen popped up and two cheerful, animated cats began to frolic across the screen.

"Whozzit?" came a sleepy reply.

He tapped his credentials from his watch to the screen. "Talbot Singh, I represent the Mill family, Jahn's grandparents. I want to ask—"

"Fuck off."

Talbot couldn't help but chuckle. "I only need a minute of your time."

"We told you guys everything."

"I'm not protocol. I'm private, hired by Jahn's mom and grandmother."

There was a moment's silence. He knew they were running his credentials. Not much would show up.

"We don't know anything."

"Okay, but I just want to ask you about Jahn. The protocol were not exactly helpful."

"'Cause they don't fuckin care." Another moment of silence. Talbot watched the cartoon cats play on the screen. "Okay, Mister. Come up, but you pull any shit and you'll be carried out in a bag."

"Understood."

Talbot straightened up and waited for the door to buzz. A second later it jingled and he pulled it open. A short elevator ride later he was standing in a long, over-lit hallway, gently knocking on a door. It swung open and a petite, black-haired woman stood in the doorway. She was aiming what appeared to be a tasing device at him.

"Get in, stand there. You move any sudden like and I'll fry your ass."

Talbot shuffled in keeping his hands at his sides, his expression as blank as he could manage. As he entered he took in what he could, but the room behind the woman was dark, the blinds apparently down. The woman stood in a pool of light from a bare projector in the ceiling. She shook only slightly as she leveled the gun.

"Jahn's grandmum hire you?"

"Yes."

"What for?"

"To find Jahn."

"You some sort of detective?"

"Yes, an assist. I think here they call me the polish."

"Dunno, man." Talbot noticed her hands shaking a bit more. The taser was getting heavy.

"Can I sit maybe, or both of us. I promise you I'm not going to—"

"Bent wire fuck, stand up! Ask what you want, be quick, or maybe my finger will slip."

"Look, I don't think there is any reason—"

"They grabbed her on the way to the fuckin bathroom!"

A new voice came from the darkness. "We haven't been out in days. Lisa won't let us."

"Shut up," she said, not taking her eyes off of Talbot, but clearly talking to the girl behind her.

"Why not, Lisa?" Talbot asked the girl with the taser.

"Tell him about the guy."

"What guy, Lisa?" Talbot asked.

"He had weird, white hair," the roommate told him.

"Hey! Stop talking to him, all clear?" Lisa demanded.

"He should know if Jahn's grandmum hired him."

"We ain't telling him shit!"

"He had totally white hair and spoke with some weird accent."

"It's called a lisp!" Lisa's arms were now shaking violently.

Talbot took a deep breath. "Hey, it's okay. I understand you're worried. Someone snatched Jahn, but it's pretty rare."

"Not the snatching, bent wire!" Lisa said, her voice cracking. "Someone saw us with Jahn and now they're going to try and snatch us too."

"What makes you—"

"The man," the voice from behind Lisa said softly.

Lisa rolled her eyes. "He knows about the man, dontcha, Mister?" she spat the words out.

Talbot shook his head.

"Sure you do. Probably here to finish the job. I should just fry you now. I got this thing fully set, Mister. Know what this'll do you your brain?"

"Okay, look, I'm gonna go. But maybe you should have your parents come take you back home. Take some time off, get away."

"So you can track us back to family?" Lisa was screaming now, her hands violently swinging back and forth, tears were rolling out of her eyes, her breathing ragged.

"I'm gonna go now, okay? Just let me open the door." Talbot felt behind him for the handle and felt relieved when his hand closed over it. "Gonna open the door and leave, okay?"

Lisa had stopped shouting but was heaving breaths and the taser, now still, was only a few inches from his head.

"I oughta end it here, asshole," she said with sudden calmed, which made Talbot's neck hairs stand up. He had the door halfway open. "I could send a message to them, send your dead body back."

Talbot could not help himself. He stopped momentarily. "To who Lisa? Who?"

The next second was a blur as he instinctively ducked down as fast as he could. He saw the taser flash and blinding white light surround him. He felt as if he was being forcibly pushed by something like a subway car into the hallway. The world went black.

Talbot heard voices before he felt anything.

"Oh fuck, I've killed him."

"No, no, look, he's breathing. The taser must have hit the door. Fuck Lisa, that thing could have killed him. Look what it did when it missed."

"Fuck. I should hit him again, direct, finish it off."

No! Talbot screamed in his head, unable to get his mouth to respond. His body lay there on the floor.

"No," the gentle voice said. "Come on, Lisa. Back inside. If he has half a brain left he'll get out."

"He'll call the protocol," Lisa sounded worried.

"He won't. What will he say? We'll tell them he was stalking. Come on, let me fix some tea. We'll figure out what's next."

Talbot heard the door close. He lay there for a few minutes, half expecting to hear the girl's door reopen or to hear another door on the hall open, but it was quiet. After a few minutes he tried his hands and they moved. Slowly he tried the rest of his body and was able to push himself into a sitting position. He sat there for a moment and then opened his eyes.

The hallway swam into view. As he tried to recall what had happened. The taser must have missed him and hit the door frame, causing the electrical field to go around him. Enough of the charge must have hit him to push him out of the apartment. His tongue felt fuzzy. Hell, he was lucky he was alive.

With great effort he pulled himself up. Unsteady and using the wall, Talbot made his way down the hallway to the elevator. He punched the button and though to look at his watch, afraid it was fried. To his relief the screen flickered to life. The rubber casing must have protected it.

The screen showed the address of the third girl, a dorm on the main campus. He sighed, his insides lurching as if he might be sick. Not the best frame of mind and body to try and figure out how to contact her, but he was running out of time. And people to talk to.

As Talbot walked away from the building he found his gait getting better with each step, but his head was still pounding. He knew the Medrac would cost too much; he would have to tough this one out. He did stop for a drink: a tall, electric green bottle of life juice. It tasted like sugar. He drank it in one go without stopping. It helped, a little.

As he walked back to the uni campus he wondered about what the two girls had told him. They had been visited by someone, someone who must have spooked them pretty badly. If Jahn had been snatched by some sort of serial killer or someone like that the person would most likely not return to try and track down friends or even people they thought might be witnesses. It might be traffickers, but they usually didn't come back to track down people connected to the taken.

Then again, the girls did seem fairly strung out. Maybe they imagined the man or maybe it had been protocol or even uni security doing follow up. Talbot knew there was something there, but he didn't have enough pieces yet. Which is why, when he got to the uni he was even more determined to speak to the third girl.

He stood outside the bland, fortress-like dorm for a moment.

There was, from what he could tell, only one way in. There probably was a back way, but Talbot was pretty sure that was alarmed and had plenty of surveillance on it. It was getting late and there was no quick way around it; Talbot would have to bluff his way in. He walked through the sliding glass doors into a fairly large vestibule. A revolving door was letting students in and out, one at a time, after they swiped their badges. Talbot watched for a moment and then approached one of the small video screens.

A pleasant, virtual face appeared. "May I help you today?"

Talbot said the name of the student and that he wanted to speak to her.

"One moment please while I ring that student. Contacting the student is not an indication that the student resides in this or any university living space." The face went dark then reappeared a moment later. "There is no response. I can try again in a few minutes, would you like me to do this?"

Talbot said yes and stood back from the screen. A few students went by. Some looked at him briefly, but most ignored him. He was careful not to go near the doors or to look at any of the students. He did not need someone calling security. After a few minutes the face reappeared and Talbot went back up to the screen.

"I'm sorry, but the student is not responding to the call. Thank you."

The screen went blank, but Talbot knew that it was still there, in a way.

"Can I leave a message?"

"I'm sorry, that is not possible."

"Why not?"

"I cannot confirm the presence of said student, accepting a message might confirm. The university respectfully suggest that you contact the student directly." The screen went black again.

"I don't actually have…look, I just want to leave contact info."

The face popped back up, the artificial smile gone. "I'm sorry I cannot help you. But I suggest that you contact the student through personal communications. If you do not have the student's personal interface then you should not attempt to contact the student."

"I just need to ask."

"I'm sorry, I cannot help you. Campus security has been alerted, perhaps they can be of assistance. Good day."

Talbot swore and turned. He did not think that the campus security would be of any help and probably, based on his earlier encounter at the security office, would just result in them calling protocol. He walked as quickly but as calmly as he could to the other side of the street and stood in the doorway of a building to watch. The security came within about three minutes. Not bad, he thought. Suddenly he was aware of someone standing around the corner of a small kiosk near him that sold sandwiches. The kiosk was closed.

"She's gone, left the next day for home." Talbot recognized the voice as Lisa's roommate. She kept herself hidden behind the kiosk. "Lisa and I should have split too, but Lisa said no."

"You always do what Lisa says?"

"Maybe. Just not now."

"Why? Where is Lisa?"

"At home asleep. She needed to crash. I just…helped her. I'll be back before she wakes up."

A young woman about five and half feet came around the corner. She was painfully thin with jet black hair and soft cinnamon skin. In normal circumstances she might have been a beauty, but after spending several days awake, paranoid, and wearing the same clothes she looked like a waif.

Talbot stuck his hand out and stepped forward. The girl initially recoiled slightly and then reached her hand out. Talbot thought it was like shaking air, the girl's hand was so light.

"Talbot Singh," he said.

"Deesee Lee." She withdrew her hand and wrapped her arms around her body.

Talbot asked softly, "So, why did you follow me?"

"I knew you'd go here next. I mean, I knew that if you really were hired by Jahn's grandma, you'd know there was another girl, right?"

Talbot nodded slightly.

"Well, so I figured it was a way to check you out."

Talbot waited again, but the girl was quiet. "So did I check out?"

Deesee nodded and bit her lip.

"So Deesee, you wanna tell me what's really going on? Why is Lisa so messed up?"

"It's that guy who came to visit us two days ago, the one with the shaved head."

"I thought you said he had white hair."

"He does but one side is shaved off. Weird style."

"What did he want?"

"Asked if we knew Jahn. Just like that, right off."

"What did you say?"

"Lisa told him we barely knew her, met her that night."

"What did he do?"

"Nothing. I mean it was weird; he said nothing, just turned and left."

"Why didn't you guys leave, like your friend here?"

"Lisa said no, where could we go? If we went back to our parents, either place, the guy might track us."

"Deesee, that's not why you guys are worried, is it?"

She looked down at the pavement.

"How long did you know Jahn Deesee?"

"Since first day here. We've been pretty close since then. Were."

"And Lisa?"

"Not until this year, couple of months. I was Jahn's best friend." She said the last part so quietly Talbot almost couldn't hear it.

"Look," Talbot said, coming closer to Deesee, "if Jahn was snatched then you have nothing to worry about. She'll resurface on another level. People I know are looking for her metrics. It's only matter of time before they pop up on a system someplace."

"She wasn't people snatched, Mister. She's not in some play room on level 62."

"How do you know this Deesee? What else is there? Do you know who snatched her?"

"No!" Deesee said so loudly it startled both herself and Talbot. "No" she repeated softly. "I swear, I don't know, I really don't."

But Talbot could hear something in her voice. "What's going on? Did Jahn tell you anything? Anything about her grandfather,

Mr Mill?"

Deesee's head shot up and she stared at him wide-eyed. Talbot could feel his chest tingle as adrenaline rushed through his body—he had opened the tiniest of cracks.

"You know him?" Deesee asked slowly.

"Did, sort of. He's dead. Jahn didn't say anything?"

Deesee shook her head.

Talbot did the timeline in his head. It was only two days after Mill had been shot that Jahn disappeared. Maybe she hadn't processed his death yet? How close could Deesee and Jahn have been for Deesee not to know this?

"Did she seem troubled?"

Deesee nodded. "She would talk about him, her grandfather. She seemed nervous, but she never mentioned he was dead. It's weird." Talbot waited, trying to hide his impatience. "I guess if I think about it, she seemed out of it that night."

"What did she talk about with her grandfather? I understand they were close."

Deesee's expression was a blend of revulsion and incredulity. "Close? Some lag, Abe!"

Talbot smiled. He wasn't familiar with the slang but was pretty sure she'd called him stupid. "Her grandmum said she hung out with her grandad a lot, so I just—"

"Seriously, Mister? Hung out? He was a fucking monster."

Talbot felt a chill and his smile faded. It was becoming a bit clearer, as if through a fogged glass. "Sorry. I had no idea."

"No, he was good about hiding it. But Jahn told me. She told me all about it, how much he hurt her but at the same time made her think he was the only one in the world who could help her. The things he would do…the awful things and how he treated her. But she couldn't see that, could she? No matter how hard I tried." Deesee was now crying softly, her voice cracking. "All I wanted to do was to help her, to love her the way she should be loved. I tried so hard to help her, but every step we took he would find a way to undo it. She needed to get away, to get out…I just wanted to help."

Talbot stood there, unsure what to do next. The wheels were turning, but he still couldn't fit the pieces together. "Deesee, I want to find Jahn and I think that there may be some connection to her grandfather's murder."

"He was murdered?" Deesee asked, more curious than alarmed.

"Yes, he was shot in his shop. But I need to know: did Jahn ever talk about anything to do with her grandfather?"

Deesee stood there, biting her lip, clearly torn.

"You can tell me Deesee, I know that the man with white hair freaked you and Lisa out for a reason. Why would people come looking for friends of Jahn after she disappeared?"

Deesee looked stubbornly at the pavement. Then she sighed. "Jahn told me that her grandfather was a smuggler."

"Smuggler of what?"

She shrugged. "I dunno. What is there? He was a jeweler, maybe of jewels."

Talbot smiled. It was actually refreshing to talk to someone who did not know the ins and outs of crime. "Probably not. Most jewels are manufactured. There's just no need. But drugs, other goods…," And people, he thought. But that seemed far-fetched, and he did not want to add to Deesee's paranoia.

"Do you think he got killed because he was smuggling?"

"Maybe, chances are."

"And so they snatch Jahn because they think she knows something?" Deesee said more to herself than Talbot.

He nodded. "Did she know anything?"

Deesee shrugged again. "I dunno. She never told me more than little bits. Hell, I don't even know what he smuggled."

"Anything else she told you? Had anyone been following her, harassing her?"

Deesee shook her head and then looked at her watch. "I gotta go now. Lisa will wake up soon."

"Okay, thanks." Talbot said, reaching out his hand. Deesee did not put hers out. "Look, a couple of things. First, if you remember anything else give me a call." He tapped his phone and hers lit up briefly. "Don't use text, only voice, and don't leave a message, okay?" She nodded. "Second, I think you and Lisa should go to a distant relative's pad? Maybe not your parents' but someplace. Lisa's gonna lose her mind, if she hasn't already."

"Okay, I think I can get us out."

"Oh, and Deesee, I wouldn't tell Lisa about any of this. The less she knows the safer she is."

Deesee nodded then turned and left. The streets were filling up with late afternoon shoppers and people returning from work. Talbot looked at his watch; it was almost time to meet Aria.

CHAPTER EIGHT

By the time Talbot walked to Aria's flat it was after six. She buzzed him in quickly, as if she had been waiting by the screen. When he walked into the apartment she grabbed him and planted her lips onto his. Quickly and without words they undressed each other. Talbot could feel the heat and passion pouring out of Aria as if she was on fire. They never made it to the bedroom. Their lovemaking was brief but intense.

Afterwards, as they sat on the couch, Talbot started to chuckle. "So much for breaking it off."

Aria arched her eyebrow. "So you think it's back on?" she asked, unsmiling.

Talbot's smile faded for a moment but then flared back up. "Very funny."

Aria laughed, a twinkle in her eyes. Talbot felt himself unwind just a small fraction but then mentally put the brakes on. He knew he should be careful, someone like Aria was above his level, in so many ways.

"So why the rushed meeting? Not just to screw me silly right?"

"So modest, Tal. But, no, not really. When I found out the girl was missing so soon after Mill's death I was worried. It seems a bit too coincidental. Mr. Mill's is killed and within 48 hours his granddaughter goes missing."

Talbot said nothing. On the way over to her apartment, he had already decided not to tell Aria about his afternoon until he had more concrete information. "So what did you find out?" he asked.

"I haven't pulled in big guns yet, so not much. The protocol here is very prickly. Not exactly eager to work on a case of a missing student. Atlanta is the largest uni for many levels, certainly down and even until you get to the high 50s."

"You been to the 50s?"

"No, but I hear. Anyway, they were not helpful."

"Any witnesses?" Talbot was fishing, to see what she might know.

"They didn't find any. Not sure they even looked."

"So, what next then?"

"Well, wait, what did you find?"

"Uh, same, really. Talked to campus security, worse than protocol."

"Really?"

"Wouldn't be surprised if I have a tag on me. Was told not to come back."

Aria laughed.

"What?"

"Like they can tag you! Small badges, small dicks. Well, no worries. We can pull files in the morning, do some cross filtering, see who she took classes with, and find out if she had friends. Everyone had friends, right?"

"Right." Talbot got up and went to the small kitchen, hoping his face had not given anything away.

"Drink?" He called back.

"Fruit juice. There's a mix in the fridge. And beer, help yourself. I picked up that Niger beer you like so much."

Talbot smiled. She was trying. He got out a glass and poured the fruit juice into it. The drink was a neon green. He made a face.

"I saw that," Aria called from the couch. "It's good; you get used to it. Full of stuff that's supposed to help your body thrive. Probably mostly sugars."

"Unlike beer," Talbot said, handing her a glass and then popping the cap off a bottle of beer, "which is just yeasts piss."

"After they eat sugar," Aria smiled.

Talbot remained standing, looking around. The apartment was probably twice as large as his parents' and that was just the entryway, kitchen, and living area. Off to the side was the main bedroom and the other side held a smaller bedroom and bath.

"It's not much," Aria said lightly, watching Talbot take in the apartment.

"Maybe not up on 34, but on 29 this is a palace. Why hang onto it?"

"Well, father died about two years ago. He owned free and clear. I was the only heir. So there is no rush to sell it. It's nice to have a place to—"

"Escape to?"

"I was going to say come to unwind, but okay. The uni has

offered me a good sum, but I don't know."

"I'd sell it. But then again, I bet the uni would give you more for this place than most buildings on 29."

Aria stood up. The blanket she had wrapped around her fell off. Talbot had to admit she looked pretty amazing: healthy, fleshy. She traced a small pattern on his shoulder.

"You need to get over this level hang up Talbot."

"It's not a hang up, it's a defense."

"Against what?" she asked, almost whispering as she put her lips near his ears. He could feel her whole body press against his.

"Against being used as a plaything."

Aria laughed softly. "Please Tal, you are hardly the victim here."

"No?"

"No. We're both adults having some fun. Come on, I think you're ready to have more fun."

Talbot woke up the next morning alone. He showered and got dressed. He found some leftover dinner from the night before in the fridge and warmed it up. As he was waiting he checked his watch. There was a message from Aria.

Crossed files, found several contacts, will send someone over. Come back tomorrow.

Talbot hoped Deesee had taken his advice. Tomorrow, huh? Why not tonight? He tried not to read too much into that.

He wandered around the apartment, which was littered with books. Talbot wondered why anyone would when you could pull up anything on your watch instantly. There were also some paintings and sculptures. All seemed to be from students, often with little inscriptions. Several empty picture frames lay about as well, their screens turned off. For a place that her father had lived in for years there seemed to be very little personal about it. And no sign of Aria's presence at all.

Talbot finished eating and left the apartment. He knew he had to go back to 29 and visit Jenson and speak to Geertz. He was halfway to the lift down when his watch buzzed. He flicked it and a small screen popped up. The face of Deesee stared at him impassively.

"You're a real boner Singh." She said, her eyes narrowing.

"What for?"

"You send those protocol around?"

"Shit. Are you still there?"

"No."

"Where."

"Nice try, bent wire."

"I didn't send protocol. They probably looked at Jahn's class list. How many classes you take with her?"

He could see Deesee frown. Talbot wanted to shout at her. If Lisa was too paranoid, Deesee seemed to be not paranoid enough. "If you're not in the flat how do you know anyone came by?"

Deesee snickered. "I guess you didn't cross those class lists, bucko. Jahn and I did take lots of shit together. We're both programming majors. I got that place wired, I 'll know if someone walks by in the hallway, much less if they break the fuckin door down and storm in, which they did."

Talbot swore to himself. What had Aria told the protocol on 31?

"Look Deesee, I have to go back to 29. Unless you think of anything don't call me. I think people are tapping my lines."

"No shit, brain master. Do you know how many taps you have on your line?"

Talbot's shock registered on his face. "No."

"Good luck with your slug life, hero." The screen went blank.

Talbot swore and broke into a run for the lift.

Talbot pounded on Jenson's door. An angry face appeared on the screen next to it.

"You're a dead man, Singh," he snarled.

"Let me in, fuckwad."

The door buzzed and Talbot stepped in. He felt cold metal to his temple and out of the corner of his eye saw Jenson standing there is his underwear.

"I'd blow yer head clean off right now, Singh, save Geertz some time. But he likes your ass for some reason. You stay here. You try to run and I will cut your legs off."

"Just get Geertz."

Talbot took a sharp blow to his stomach.

"Bitch," Jenson said and went back into his flat, closing the door. A moment later it reopened and Talbot got up and moved to the door. Jenson pushed him back—hard.

"Say what you gotta say. Geertz can hear."

Talbot straightened up and pulled his shirt down. "Sorry to bother you, Geertz, but there have been developments."

"Go on." Geertz said.

"I talked to two of the girls. The other one is gone, went home maybe."

"Yes, home."

Talbot wanted to roll his eyes, they could have told him this before. "Anyway, the other two, not happy to see me, said someone had been by, asking questions."

"Who?"

"They didn't know. They thought protocol or maybe the snatcher gang."

"Negative to both. Definitely not protocol and I track no gang activity related to the missing girl. No clues as to who it was, Singh?"

"No, but it freaked them out. One of them tased me."

"And you lived?"

"She missed."

"Clearly. Go on."

"I also got a message from Aria."

"Yes, we know. She's back?"

Talbot wanted to scream, what else did Geertz know that he wasn't sharing? "She wants to reopen Mill, and it's probably a good idea. I also talked to one of the girls for a long time who found me after I recovered from the tase. She told me that Jahn and her grandfather had a, uh, relationship, and that Mill was some sort of smuggler."

"Smuggler? Of what?"

"She had no idea. I thought you might know?"

"No idea, Mr. Singh. Does Detective Olsen think it is still

Treasure?"

"She didn't say. She just thought there might be a connection and wanted to help."

"Did she send the protocol over to the girls this morning?"

"Pretty sure. I got a call from one of the girls about 9:30 asking if I had done it."

"You got a call?"

"Yeah, about 9:30." Talbot wondered why this was news to Geertz.

"Interesting. We need to meet briefly, Mr. Singh."

"Sure, should I stay here or—"

"See you soon. Go home, Mr. Singh or wherever. It doesn't matter. Show him out, Jenson."

"With pleasure." Jenson stepped around Talbot and opened the door. Talbot slid carefully by and outside before Jenson brought his knee up into Talbot's groin. Talbot doubled over onto the sidewalk. Jenson spat, the spit landing on Talbot's shirt.

"When this is all done, Singh, and Geertz has no use for you, I'm gonna find you and string you up by your balls until you die."

The door slammed and Talbot lay there for a moment.

Thirty minutes later Talbot came out of the Medrac feeling much better. The persistent headache from the tasing was finally gone. As he stepped across the street a tall man fell in step along side of him. He did not need to look up.

"All better?"

"No thanks to your goon."

"Yes, sorry about that. Jenson is a faithful lapdog, but like all dogs he can bite. Come into this store with me."

Geertz led him into a small card shop, filled to the brim with note cards, stuffed animals, and leafy green plants. As they entered an elderly woman behind the counter smiled, which faded quickly when she saw Geertz. Without a word she quickly moved from the behind the counter and through a door on the side. As it closed behind her Talbot looked around and realized they were alone in the shop.

Geertz stepped around a large tower of small plants with bows around their pots. The air was humid and smelled…strange. Talbot could not put his finger on it what it was.

"Decay, Mr. Singh. The smell, it is decay, in the dirt, of plants. They mix in dead plants to supplement the soil. This way the new plants feed off the dead plants. A pleasant smell though, no?"

"Uh, sure."

"Here, take this." Geertz held out a small, black card. It was the shape of a transit card, but there were no logos or other markings on it.

"What is this?"

"It's magic," Geertz said, smiling for the first time that Talbot could recall. "A gift to you from me. A token, as it were. It's a multi-pass transit card, but much more than an MTC. It's an EMTC—everlasting—programmed to switch between several million users accounts. It deducts trips from all sorts of cards, both legit and not so legit. So, in essence, it will always have money on it to get you where you need to go."

Talbot hesitated.

"Go on, Mr. Singh. You are already in deep; this will not drag you under any further."

Talbot took the card. The matte black finish did not reveal any of its secrets. "Any level?"

"Certainly, Mr. Singh. Within reason. I think a trip as far up as one can go would trigger alarm bells, however. Take a trip up to the 40s for a day, on me, but after that use it for business only."

Talbot let himself dream for a split second. "Thank you all the same, but I need to track down Jahn first."

"Honorable, also pragmatic. I have scanned the circuits again for our missing young lady. No sign of her. It would be helpful if I had her biometrics."

"I could ask her mother, but I thought those could be altered."

"Eventually, yes, but it takes a few hours. Until that point happened we would have more of a trail."

"So no ideas?"

"Mr. Singh, I have plenty of ideas but no, nothing to tell you."

"Well, as long as we're on the subject, it seems like you know a lot of things you don't tell me."

"Don't be presumptuous, Mr. Singh. I know far more than you will ever know. It is my job to know things. Besides which, I dare say you too are holding back things."

Talbot felt color rise in his cheeks. "Like what?"

"How did you know about the protocol this morning? Did Detective Olsen tell you?"

"No, you saw her message right? I knew she might."

"Then how?"

"When Deesee called me—Jahn's friend—she called me... holy shit—you don't know about her call?"

"I see nothing there. Mr. Singh. No calls to or from your watch all morning. Yet you say you spoke with her?"

"I spoke and saw her pop up display."

"Fascinating. Well, Mr. Singh, please don't let this...glitch, mislead you. We want to be kept informed. Is that clear?"

"Yes, of course."

"Good." Geertz rapped on the counter hard and the elderly woman came tumbling out from behind the door. He then turned to Talbot, winked, and left the shop. Talbot moved to follow him.

"Buy a plant," the woman said. It was not a suggestion. Talbot glanced at her in surprise and when he turned back Geertz had disappeared, lost in the street. "Mr. Geertz would want you to buy one, sonny."

"Okay." Talbot hastily picked out a small plant. Coughing, the woman shook her head and pointed to a slightly larger and more expensive one next to it. Talbot smirked, picked it up, and waved his watch over the counter. The receipt popped up and the woman handed it to him.

"Thirty-day guarantee. The pot has a water alarm; it'll beep when you need to water it. Now, scram." Her voice was bland but her eyes were hard.

Talbot nodded and quickly left the shop.

Back at his parents' apartment Talbot sat at the small kitchen counter looking at the card Geertz had given him. He was sorely tempted to take the card and ride up as far as he could, just to say he had. But he knew a little bit about what Geertz had warned about.

The higher up you went the more scrutiny you came under. Rumor was that past level 60 they scanned your ID before they let you off, no matter what kind of money you had on your transit card. Still, a vacation in the 40's would be nice.

He turned the card over in his hands, wondering about Mr. Mill. If he had been a smuggler then what exactly was he smuggling? As far as he knew, Mr. Mill had just been a small-time jeweler. He probably never even left the level...

"Shit!"

Talbot bolted up and ran out of the apartment. He bounded down the stairs instead of using the elevator. He stopped in front of Mrs. Mill's apartment and counted to 10 to calm himself then gently knocked. Her daughter answered the door. She looked strung out. Her red eyes looked momentarily hopeful but then reading Talbot's face she looked away.

"Momma's not here," Jessica said.

"It's okay. Can I ask you a couple of questions? I don't even need to come in."

"It's okay, come in."

Talbot entered the apartment, which was shabbier and less clean than his parents' place. If Mr. Mill had been smuggling it must not have paid well. He turned to Jessica.

"I just need to know a couple of things. Mrs. Mill mentioned you moved up."

"Yes, we live on 31. Jahn was about 10 when we moved there."

Talbot had to put a mental picture of a 10-year-old Jahn and her grandfather out of his head. "And your dad would come up to visit?"

"Sure."

"How often?"

"Dunno…every few months. Why?"

"Just trying to put the puzzle together. Did your mother come too?"

"Not usually. Truth is, he used to come up and take Jahn out to the park or the arcade, like just for the afternoon. That was about it."

"Thanks. I don't have anything to tell you but the moment I do—"

"My father was a good man," she interrupted. Talbot caught himself.

"Yes, of course," Talbot said impassively and stood to leave.

"He's dead Talbot; leave him in peace," she said, looking at him directly.

"Jessica, is there anything else you'd like to tell me?"

A silence hung in the air then Jessica slowly shook her head. "Just bring her back to me, Talbot, and everything will be alright. He's dead now."

Talbot left the building unsure what to do with this new bit of information, but things were looking darker and darker for Mr. Mill. He made his way over a few streets to a small protocol station. His relief was palpable when he walked in and saw an old friend of his sitting at the main desk.

"Well, looks like protocol is desperate leaving you in charge, Henry!" he said, forcing joviality.

A heavyset man who looked like he had spent a lifetime eating too much looked up with hooded eyes. "Come to turn yourself in,

Singh? Had enough of being a corpse chaser?"

"Never, fucker! How's it going?" Talbot asked with a wide grin.

The man also smiled and held up a hand. "All is well my friend, all is well. Still on the assist beat?"

"Of course, always."

"Well, if you ever want honest work come work for us. I can put in a good word, erase your record."

"If I want honest work I certainly won't come here!" They both laughed. "But seriously, Henry, I do need a small favor."

"Oh Lord, here it comes. Great swoops Tal, why don't you buy a guy a drink before you bend him over and fuck him senseless?"

"Not my style. Seriously, all I need to know is someone's transit records."

"All?! Why stop there? Maybe you'd like their fuckin first born too?"

"It's Mill, Henry. I need it for Mr. Mill."

Henry's smile faded. "Shit, Tal…make it difficult for me, will yah. Isn't that case open?"

"Shouldn't be. It was closed."

"Already?"

"Yeah, should be."

Henry frowned and began to tap away at a small screen that popped up out of the desk. "Shit, you're right. That was fast. Okay, makes it a little easier. What do you need exactly?"

"Last two years—no, three years—anyplace he went."

"Anyplace? Come on, Tal, I'm good, but…"

"Okay, any lifts up. Can you add in down too?"

Henry grimaced but said nothing. He swiveled the screen around.

"I don't see any records?" Talbot said.

"No shit. They ain't there yet. It's an information request form."

"Oh come on, Henry. If I wanted to do it that way I would have used online."

"Tal, I'm not going to get my ass in a sling just 'cause you want to know every time Mill took a crap."

A piece of paper popped out of the desk. Henry's meaty hand came down on it. "The form is for you to sign," Henry said, his eyes locked on Talbot's.

Talbot looked down and saw a second piece of paper underneath the form. He carefully palmed the second sheet and then handed back the first sheet.

"Fuck you very much, Henry. I'm not signing anything."

"Then no way, Tal. Sorry, them's the rules."

"You've changed, man."

"You haven't. Get lost, fucker. And you owe me a beer."

"Why?"

"For not arresting your ass."

"For what?"

"I dunno, but you still owe me!"

Talbot smiled at him then turned and left with a look of rejection. He walked several blocks before he retrieved the second sheet of paper from his pocket. The small, neat print showed the dates and times of Mr. Mill's lift rides for the past three years. Each was to level 31.

CHAPTER NINE

Talbot could barely sleep that night. He scoured the information net most of the night, looking, searching. By the time his mother and father were up he had a list of about eight girls, all from the uni. He knew he had to see Aria as soon as he could.

"Did you sleep, Tal?" his mother asked.

"Slept fine, Mom."

"Don't bullshit me, boy. It's not healthy. Get some rest."

"Soon, Mom, soon. I'll be back tomorrow."

His mom's eyes went wide. "You got a girl?"

"Not now, Mom, but yeah. Gotta go."

"Be careful!" she called out as he left the flat.

Talbot made his way to the lift for 34 and flashed the black card, half expecting security to jump on him as he did but the gate slide open soundlessly. He went into the waiting lift car and sat down. He carefully tucked the card into his pants pocket. He tried to focus on what he had to tell Aria, but his mind kept wandering to the idea that he could, if he wanted, explore every level now.

The lift left 29 and arrived at 34 a few minutes later. Talbot got off and made his way down to the protocol station. This time he did not risk actually calling on Aria, but instead used his watch. He figured that he had nothing to lose; clearly Geertz could track his card use and know that he had gone to 34. And why else would he go?

He messaged Aria and then made his way over to a small park near the station. He noticed for the first time that here on 34 they used real trees as the uni did on 31. He resisted the urge to touch the tree and instead stood there looking at the leaves. A passing delivery cart stirred up a small breeze and he watched the leaves briefly dance in the wind. The effect, he thought, was magic.

It was no more than five minutes before Aria was standing next to him, wearing an eager and expectant expression. Talbot hoped he would not let her down.

"Hi," he said sheepishly.

"Hi, what have you got?" She sounded brisk, almost business-like.

"So, I got to thinking about Mill and his granddaughter: how she lived and eventually went to school on 31."

"Okay."

"So I, uh, pulled Mill's transport record."

"I know."

"You know?"

He could see Aria flush slightly. "Yes. Not a big deal but his file has a pull alarm. I got a report last night. I figured it was you when I saw the precinct."

"Shit, I hope I didn't get Henry in trouble."

"No, don't worry. I'm the only one the report went to. You should have asked."

"I know, I know, but I got excited. Look, I got his transit use, all the time he left 29. And he went to 31 every time."

"To visit the girl?"

"Maybe. Look, I did some research about missing people from the uni over the past few years. That is this list. Eight people in the past three years. All girls. Those are the ones I could find in the news. It's weird no one put this together, eight missing girls—"

"Out of the 46,000 students that go there each year, Tal? It's probably higher. We should pull records."

"Can you do that?"

"Maybe, I guess. Why?"

"Look, for all eight of these girls they line up to within 24 hours of Mill being on 31."

"But he was on 31 dozens of time a year."

"Okay, but a pretty big coincidence that he is on 31 within a day of each girl disappearing, no?"

Aria looked at the paper for a moment. "I'd want to pull records, see if there are others, see if they match up. What are you thinking? Is Mill a killer?"

"None of these girls have ever shown up, even as bodies."

"Absence does not prove death."

"I know, I know, but the pattern."

"Okay, so maybe we have something here. Off the top of my head I see some issues: Why was Mill killed? Why was it a gang-style hit that may not even be a gang hit? And how did his granddaughter get disappeared? If he's a killer and he's dead…"

"Yeah, a few holes, I know."

"Look, Tal, I'll pull what I can and meet you at the apartment on 31 tonight after 6:00. Here's a key." She tapped her watch and his watch lit up. He looked up, surprised.

"What? It makes it easier," she smiled and kissed him on the lips. "See you at six!"

He tried to play it as cool as he could, getting to the flat building at five of six but then waiting a few minutes afterwards to ring the bell.

"I thought I gave you the key," Aria's voice rang out.

He smiled and swiped his watch over the screen. The door clicked open. Inside Aria was smiling, but less eager to see him than the previous time. She had a serious demeanor about her.

"I pulled stuff," she said. "And three more girls came up that matched travel dates with Mr. Mill."

"And?"

"And we have a body. Two of the girls are still missing, but the third girl was found, get this, on level eight. Level eight!"

"But there's no record of Mill being that low."

"No, but he's a smuggler right? Look, I don't know, but that's nine girls who match up to Mill's travel dates. It suggests some sort of connection."

"Why would that one girl end up on eight?"

"No idea. I have a call into protocol down there."

"At least they have protocol there…They do, right?"

"Yes, they do—for what it's worth."

"What about the other eight girls, anything on them?"

"Well, it was difficult, I don't want to trip some sort of alarm. But I."

"Why not?"

Aria paused. "We don't know anything yet, really, do we? It could be just a terrible coincidence. Or it could be that he was a serial killer. But until we know what's going on I don't want half the department to know we're sniffing around."

"Okay, I'll bite—why not? So we chase down a dead end."

"I keep forgetting you're not protocol. Tal, listen: why do you think polish like you exist? You do your stuff for a client, right? Your clients expect results. But protocol is different; its administration."

"Okay, but you guys still have a job to do."

"But it's not the job you think, baby. The job is to play along to get along. To make sure we've filled out the right forms, cc'd the correct people. If, along the way, we solve something, all the better."

"Okay, so just fill out some forms."

"Sure, Tal, but what if we're wrong? Opening an investigation that is a dead end or reopening a closed case and end up with nothing—that's not playing by the rules; that's creating work, creating uncertainty. People above will ask: What is she up to? Is she stupid or is she trying to make us look bad by chasing down cases? Either way, I look bad; either way, I get pegged as a problem."

"So we just forget about it then?"

"No, not at all. You're not understanding me. We do as much as we can on our own. If we think we have a case, we go back and reopen the case. But only if we have enough evidence to really make things stick. At that point I go to a superior, get them involved, make them happy, I get some credit, everyone gets to announce a winner. But until then we're just causing trouble."

"Well, shit, how does anything get done with that attitude?"

Aria laughed and kissed him on the mouth lightly.

"Okay, so what did you find?" Talbot asked again.

"Nothing much. I pulled what I could. They were all uni students, but that's not surprising, so damn many of them around here. They all had different courses of study. Nothing in common I could see."

"I bet if we could run their intel through uni and protocol records we could sift out connections."

"Maybe, and we'll do that later if we can. The main problem now is that the girls are missing. Half of them for under a year." Aria got up and put her glass on the counter. She rummaged in the fridge and came back with a small bottle of synthine. "I'm not trying to say you're not onto something, but we don't have much to go on. We need some connection back to Mill or level 29 or something, even his granddaughter, to make a case."

"What about the girl on eight?"

"What about her?"

"Was there a report?"

"Yeah, pretty basic. She was found, brought in, and handed over to protocol. No signs of any trauma."

"What did she die of?"

"Not sure. Like I said, the report was pretty basic."

Talbot thought for a moment. "Wait: brought in. What do you mean: Was she brought in to the station?"

"Uh, no. I mean she was brought in from outside."

Talbot's brow knit together. "Outside of what?"

"The city. She was hanging off a ledge."

Talbot's spine bristled and every hair on his neck stood up.

"Oh man, Tal, you mean…Of course, I guess 29 probably

doesn't. Even eight doesn't really. You've never been to the edge of the city?"

Talbot shook his head slowly. He knew, of course, that the city was finite. It had an edge, maybe even a top and bottom, although that seemed less certain. Yet he had never seen the edge or thought much about it. Most of the city's circumference was air intake and handling units. At least on 29 they were set up that way.

Aria studied him like he was some sort of exotic creature in a zoo. Talbot felt distinctly uncomfortable. "What?" he finally said.

Aria tilted her head and took a long swig of synthine. "You do have a lot to learn, Tal, about the ways of the world."

"I manage fine. So I haven't been to the edge. I bet you couldn't find more than five people who have on 29. That's beside the point anyway." He was eager to change the subject away from what he didn't know and back to what neither of them knew. "Back to the girl, who found her?"

"The report doesn't say. Someone did and someone knows a bit more than what protocol put down, that's for sure."

"Crap. Does this mean I have to go down to eight and talk to people?"

"You might, yes."

"Why couldn't he have dumped the body on 68 instead?"

"It's not funny, Tal."

"I know."

"It's okay. Look, you did good. Real good. I think we're on track to figuring out some things. It's probably bigger than just Mill."

"Yes, it would have to be to explain the stray things, like Jahn disappearing after Mill dies."

"Exactly."

"Okay, I'll go to eight tomorrow."

Aria looked concerned.

"What?" Talbot asked.

"I'm not sure that's a good idea," she said softly.

"Why not? It's the only thing we have."

"Think about it, Tal. You've been to 19 right? Any lower?"

Talbot shook his head; he knew where this was going.

"Level 19 is bad enough. Now go 11 levels more? I contacted the protocol station—the protocol station, for the entire level. True, it's mostly processing plants but there are still several million down there. I'm not even sure you can get a normal lift there."

"There are lifts. Look, I can ask around, find out what I need, what to do, where to go."

"Your Treasure contacts?"

"I have lots of contacts. I'll be fine."

"I don't like it," she said, as if closing the subject.

"Aria, I'm a big boy. I can take care of myself. I have a duty to my client and to Jahn. If this helps us find her in any way…I promise I will be careful and go directly to the protocol station and come right back. You're letting your upper level paranoia get in the way."

He saw her bristle but she did not protest. "Do you have credit to get back up?" she asked. "I can give you some."

"I have enough."

She looked at him, still determined to prevent him from going.

"I promise I will come back." Talbot said, gently taking both of her hands and looking into her eyes. She sighed and he could see her eyes soften.

"Okay, fine. Tomorrow you can go down to eight and speak to protocol. I can set you up and maybe they can lead you to people who know about the girl being found. Do some detective work and then we'll meet back here tomorrow night."

"Okay. And until tomorrow?"

Aria laughed. "Come on, Tal, just kiss me already."

Talbot leaned in and all seemed right with the world.

CHAPTER TEN

The next day Talbot got up before Aria and slipped out. He wanted to make the trip down to eight as early as possible and get back as soon as possible. It was true: he had never been lower than 19. He wasn't even sure what would await him at such a low level. He knew that on some of the lower levels there was only machinery. Great engines that cleaned the air or did water filtration. Some levels, like eight he supposed, also processed the large amounts of waste flowing from the levels above. But he also knew that some levels were basically no better than wild jails. Eight would be low enough that he would have to be careful. At least there were protocol down there—a small comfort, he knew, but still a comfort.

He would make a brief stop on 19 to talk to his contacts there about eight. He wasn't sure what they could tell him or how they could help him, but it was worth a shot.

By the time he got to 19 it was barely 7:00 a.m. Commuters were lining up at the elevators and the streets were full of local level people going to work, vendors selling coffee and breakfast. This time of the day the level seemed much less threatening. Talbot wondered if it would be the same on eight. If possible he wanted to get down there before 9:00 a.m. and back before lunchtime.

He was not going to the jeweler's this time; instead he made his way directly to a small bar. Despite the early hour Talbot knew it would be open; it never closed. Ducking down a side street off the main road from the lift he found the dingy, grey door. There was no sign and no windows. Talbot wasn't even sure it had a name. The only way to know it was a bar was to know. His mentor had shown it to him one day. That was how most people found the place: friends told friends.

Inside was dark but a lot cleaner and, frankly, nicer than what the outside advertised. Small tables and benches lined the two side walls. At the back was a bar that ran the width of the fairly narrow room.

Only a few people sat in the booths. No one was at the bar except for the bartender, a stooped, older man with a bald head and a long white beard. His narrow eyes glanced at Talbot as he walked in and then went back to washing the bar top with a foul-looking rag.

"Is Round Man here?" Talbot asked when he got to the counter.

The bartender did not look up. "No one here."

Talbot was not put off. "Can you tell him Tal Singh is here? I just need intel."

The bartender still did not look up and kept wiping the bar, making his way down the length. After a moment a pleasantly rotund man came out from a door behind the bar. He wore a saffron robe and a large smile on his face.

"Tal!" he said in a booming voice. Talbot winced, not used to being called out in public, especially on 19.

"Round Man!" Talbot said, bracing for the bear hug. He had never known the man's real name.

"What can I do you for, Tal?"

"I have a case."

"Well, I figured you weren't down here for the view," Round Man laughed loudly.

"I have to go to eight."

Round Man's face slackened and his smile vanished. "Eight? You mean 18?"

"No eight."

"Why the fuck you want to go down there, Tal?" he demanded, his voice now serious.

"Not want to. Need to. I thought maybe you might have some advice."

"About eight?! No one fucking goes to eight, Tal. Want my advice? Don't go!" he laughed again, but this time not as loud. "Fuck, you serious aren't you?"

"Yes. I just need to go for an hour or so."

"Bad pace, Tal. Fuck you up fast down there. Go, come back quickly. Don't take the fucking scenic route."

Talbot waited a beat. Round Man laughed. "What?"

"That's it? I thought you were connected."

"I am, but not to fuckin eight." Round Man sighed, "Okay, look…if you get into some sort of trouble you go to Luck Dog Café, ask for man named Carl. But I gotta warn you, Tal, he's a mean pig. Just mean. But unlike others on eight, he won't kill you. Cost you a lot, but he'll help you. That's the best I can do, okay?"

"Perfect, thanks Round Man. I probably won't even need the guy."

"Best if you don't."

Talbot left the bar feeling a lot less sure of himself and his travel plans. With a pit in his stomach he made his way over to the lift. The doors swung open automatically. It was free to go down.

The first thing Talbot noticed about eight was the air. It was noticeably stale. As he walked off the lift platform and stepped out onto the street, the air hit him like a wall. However he quickly forgot about the air once he took in his surroundings. The buildings were neat, a little worn, and the style was as old as anything he'd seen on 29. Most jarring was their height; the buildings were no more than 20 feet high, maybe less.

The effect was tremendously oppressive. Between the air and the low ceiling Talbot felt as if he could not breathe. Several people milled about, seemingly unaffected. Talbot felt like screaming, or at least running back to the lift and getting back up as far as he could go, even past 29 or 31 or 34. He stood for a moment and let the anxiety wash over him. He felt sweat trickle down his back, but eventually he centered himself.

Once he was under control he took a second look around, trying very hard not to look up. But even so the horizon was so low, so close as he looked down the street, his chest tightened. To distract himself he focused on finding the street that led to the protocol station.

Things were not just compact vertically on eight. The protocol station was only a couple blocks from the lift. To get there Talbot passed through a thriving central shopping district that was thronged with people. But as he left the shops behind the street became increasingly deserted, as if the residents had been warned away. By the time he reached the station he was the only one on the street.

Inside the nondescript building, there was a long, blank concrete wall with a lone screen imbedded into the wall at eye level. As Talbot approached it a weary face appeared. He was surprised to see it wasn't a sim but a real person, his cheeks covered with stubble, his eyes bloodshot.

"What?"

"Talbot Singh here to see, uh," Talbot looked at his watch screen, "Captain Fry."

The face disappeared off screen for a moment, revealing a dingy, beige cubicle and a worn, black chair. The cubicle had no decorations of any kind. A moment later a loud buzz startled Talbot and a large metal door to his left swung open as the entrance door locked. The man from the screen poked his head out, motioned Talbot in, and led him down a long concrete hallway to another door, which buzzed open. Meant to convey security, the short walk only increased Talbot's anxiety. Inside the second door there was a tiny waiting room with two small benches. Unlike any other station waiting room Talbot had ever been to, this one was empty save for himself.

The man from the screen grunted and motioned for Talbot to sit then went to a compact intercom on the wall and pressed a button. "He's in." He then exited through a back door, leaving Talbot by himself in the room. There were no windows, only one large light array on the ceiling. The atmosphere was even more oppressive than outside and Talbot felt like he was in a small box. He silently prayed that the lights would not go off.

Minutes ticked by. He finally heard a small click and the back door swung open. A large, overly muscular man, more gorilla than human, lumbered through and stood in the doorway. Talbot stood up and found that the man was a head taller than him. Talbot wondered how the hell the guy could exist in a place with such low ceilings.

The man stuck out a meaty paw. "Fry," he said in a surprisingly soft voice.

"Singh, Talbot Singh."

"Yeah, we got word. Come on back."

Talbot followed Fry through the door and into yet another hallway. Talbot half-wondered if he could find his way out of the station if need be. Fry stopped at the first door they came to, flashed his wrist, and the door unlocked. They went in and Talbot found himself in a pleasant, well-lit room. Large video screens hung on the deep blue walls, which displayed various works of art. The effect was like a cold bucket of water.

"Wow." Talbot couldn't help himself. He had never been in a station so well appointed.

Fry let out a wry chuckle. "Not expecting this on eight, huh?"

"Not even on 29."

"Small perk for taking this crap job. Twenty-nine? I thought you were 34."

"No. Just working with someone on 34."

"Oh, that explains the directive." Fry tapped the air in front of him and a small screen opened. "Singh…supposed to give you the file on Rose Roberts. Here we go…"

He flicked the screen around so Talbot could see. It was the same file Aria had showed him the night before. "Thanks, but I've seen this," Talbot tried to sound grateful but Fry's expression seemed irked.

"What else can I tell you? Trust me buddy, we get plenty of dead here."

"Yeah? Pretty tough beat?"

"Sure, I guess. Not as bad as up on 16. I commute; this hell hole ain't fit for people. Look, we do what we're told here. And nothing else, okay? I'm sure there are lots of dead bodies floating around this joint because even though we don't exactly get out much we still seem to get plenty of them. So what's one more?"

"What is one more? Why process this girl?"

"Cause it wasn't one of their own."

"Did you know she was from the uni on 31? Atlanta?"

Fry waived his hand. "She was dead, made no difference. I fed her metrics in. Took a while, but made a match."

"How long?"

"How long what?"

"You said it took a while to match up metrics. When I go on a lift they match me up in a few seconds."

"It took a few hours. We got slow connectivity down here, maybe. She was pretty beat up too."

"Why, cause of death?"

"Maybe, who knows? Died of hypothermia."

"What is that?"

"Exposure. To the outside."

"Oh yea, I heard."

"Yeah, they found her hanging off a ledge outside. Been there for a few days they think."

"But how did she get there and down here?"

"Fuck if I know. Didn't come from here, at least there's no record. Had to come from above."

"So she fell then, died in the fall?"

"Yes and no. She probably did fall or jumped but didn't die from that. I told ya, she died from exposure. Fuck of a way to go."

"I guess so. Was there an autopsy?"

"Not so much. Medical examiner looked at her, determined the cause of death, but didn't cut her open. Parents claimed her body. No autopsy, some religious thing."

"So, nothing else then?"

"Like I said, I showed you what I got."

Talbot sat for a moment, thinking. Fry stood up. "Sorry to rush you but we do have stuff to do down here, even if it isn't much."

"One more thing: who found her? I mean, did you guys find her?"

"Naw, let's see. Brought in my municipal workers. They were checking vents most likely. Lots of shit to vent down here, you know. Literally."

"Any way I could talk to them?"

"Dunno. I can give you their names, you can call them. Your wrist should work down here well enough. But trust me, pal, these folks down here are not always the most forthcoming."

Fry tapped the screen and Talbot saw his watch flash.

"A word of warning, Singh. If you do talk to them, make it in the open. Make it on Market in front of the lift."

"Sure."

Fry led Talbot through the concrete maze to the entry vestibule. Before disappearing behind the steel door Fry stopped and turned to Talbot.

"I was serious about the meeting, Singh. We got one rule here: we don't go out there for no one. You get in trouble out there, you are on your own. Understand?"

Talbot nodded. Fry stepped behind the door and it clicked loudly in the long entryway.

Once out of the building Talbot took a moment to appreciate the relative openness of the street. After being in the concrete bunker of the protocol station, the street seemed massive and expansive.

Talbot made his way to the market area, the street helpfully called Market. He noted it was still bustling despite it now being after 9:00 a.m. He stood under an awning in front of a shop. He tapped his phone and called one of the two men given to him by Fry.

A young, confused face popped up on the small screen the watch projected. "Who is?"

"Hi, is this Alec?"

"Who is?"

"Alec, this is Talbot Singh, I wanted to talk to you about Rose."

"Wha?"

"Rose, the girl you found last year, outside."

The young man's face went from confused to slack to worried, "Fuck that business."

"I just wanted to talk to you and Jerome."

"Who is?" a second voice off-screen asked. Alec gave the unseen person a dirty look. He then turned back to the screen.

"Well sorry, no can do. Can't leave work, Mister."

"Okay, do you get lunch?"

Alec laughed. "Not to talk to some swerve from up top. You wanna talk to me, Mister, come talk to me."

"I was really hoping you could come here."

Alec laughed again; he had Talbot's number. "Afraid, top side? Upper level pussy. Look, Mister, we work in the fuckin' municipal waste plant. We ain't gonna jump yer ass at work."

Talbot hesitated. If he didn't talk to them he might lose the one last shred of information that might be useful. He was not even sure it was worth it, but if not, then he had nothing really.

"Too bad, Mister. Nice life in heaven side."

"Wait. Okay, just tell me how I get there."

"Follow your nose."

The kid was not just being flip, Talbot thought, as he came upon a grey stucco building with flat black windows. He had walked about eight blocks off Market, the stench getting worse with each step. Despite his increasing anxiety nothing bad had happened.

126

Moving away from Market the people thinned out as before, but unlike at the protocol station, there were still occasional people drifting by even when he got to the waste plant. Talbot had been to enough lower levels to know to keep your head down and walk with purpose. No one gave him a second glance.

Talbot made his way into the building under a sign that read: Level 8 Wellington District Waste Treatment Facility #12. Inside there was a large pen area with several desks. The walls were bright colors and the furniture, worn and old, was nevertheless comfortable looking. Diminutive, green plants sat on each desk and taller plants stood sentry by the front windows. Idly Talbot reached out to touch the leaves of an especially tall broad-leafed plant. A voice startled him just as he touched the cool green leaf.

"Can I help you?"

He turned to see a smartly dressed young woman who flashed a pleasant smile.

"Uhn, yes. I'm supposed to meet Alec from maintenance here?" Talbot mused for a moment as to how odd that sounded; a maintenance person in a place like this seemed redundant.

"Yes, I think Alec and Jerome are waiting for you in the break room. Come on, I'll show you."

Talbot followed the woman through the large open area, around a corner, and into a cozy space littered with couches and mismatched chairs. In the corner was a kitchenette with the smell of burnt coffee. Sprawled on one of the couches was Alec. Nervously perched on a chair nearby was another, even younger looking kid Talbot assumed was Jerome.

Both of them jumped up when the young woman marched

into the area. Jerome's eyes were on the floor, but Alec gave her a wide smile.

"Hi Jade!"

She ignored him and instead turned to Talbot with a weary look. "All yours," she said then left to go back up front.

Talbot extended his hand but Alec stuck his in his overalls. Both of the men were dressed in light blue overalls with a small insignia on the breast pocket. Alec rocked on his feet for a moment.

"Soooo, no one jumped you, eh?"

"No, they did not."

"Toldja."

"So I wanted to talk to you about the girl, the one you found."

"Yeah, pretty messed up that was. Scared the crap out of us, right Jerome?"

Jerome nodded but did not say anything.

"Can you tell me how you found her?"

"She was on a ledge. We got those on this level we're so old. Little places you might be able to sit on if yer careful and not afraid to look down."

"She was dead, right?"

"Yeah, but the protocol told me she probably wasn't the whole time."

"So, you guys went out there for…?"

"Check on filters an' things. Routine. We go out about every other week. Not just there, to all sorts of outlets we go into and check."

"Why was she there? Couldn't she come in?"

"Not hardly. All those vents are locked—from the inside,

mind you. We're not expecting people to break out exactly, are we?"

"So she just sat there…," Talbot said to himself.

"Well, probably couldn't have climbed in anyway, on account of her broken leg from the fall."

"What fall?"

Alec laughed, Jerome even cracked a smile. "Mister, how do you think she got there? Flew? She fell, from 10."

"Level 10? How do you know? She went missing from 31…"

"You fall from 31 you ain't gonna land on a ledge on 8. You land below. You never seen outside have you?"

"No. Okay, but why 10? Why not 9? Maybe she was climbing down, slipped."

"She was climbing down alright, slipped or jumped, took chance. But she was clearly from 10."

Talbot suppressed the urge to yell. "Okay, how do you know?"

"What she was wearing. It was from 10."

It was like pulling teeth. "What was?"

"Her jumpsuit. From CSA on 10. Didn't they tell you?"

"They must have forgotten." Talbot was about to ask what CSA was when he noticed Alec go pale and sweaty, Jerome looked down at the floor even harder, if possible.

Alec stammered. "Well, it was there plain as day. I told the protocol and everything, not like it was a secret. Right Jerome?" Jerome did not look up. Alec glanced around. "Say, Mister, you never seen outside?"

"No, like I said."

"Okay. Look, what do you say Jerome and I take you to the vent where we found the girl? Show you around and all?"

Talbot hesitated. Something had tripped Alec up, was he trying to change the subject or was this a move to somehow get rid of the troublesome topsider? Alec was young, but not stupid.

"You a paranoid, even for a topsider, Mister. Ain't nothing gonna happen, promise. Look, this place is crawling with cameras. Trust me."

Talbot's brain screamed, NO! "Okay, fine. It'll be interesting."

"That's the spirit."

"So, wait, if there are cameras everywhere—"

"On the inside, Mister. Like I said, most people don't try to break into 8. Come on, we can go there in the cart we brung."

CHAPTER ELEVEN

They left the open area, going through double doors into a long concrete hallway. Talbot was sensing a pattern. Parked just beyond the doors was a small truck. Talbot had never seen one inside a building or one this large. In the back bed was a large assortment of tools and boxes. The front was a small cab that would sit two comfortably. The three of them had to jam together.

"Hang on, Mister. It's a ways and this thing'll open up pretty wide on the straightaways."

The truck took off at an unnerving speed. Talbot could not recall even subway cars going this fast. Alec seems unfazed as he lightly steered the truck down the impossibly long, straight hallway. They passed no one the entire way. Every so often they would slow down and take a corner that would materialize out of thin air. Within a few moments Talbot had lost track of where they were. If Alec was to shove him out of the truck at that point, Talbot realized he might wander the halls for weeks and never find his way out.

They finally slowed down and stopped at the end of a hall in front of a set of double doors. They all hopped out. Alec ran his wrist over the door handle and it clicked open. Inside was a massive room, only about 20 feet high, but it seemed to stretch out in all directions. Great machines lined the room in neat rows, each almost as big as the truck they had left in the hall. The machines vibrated slightly, making strange hums.

"Air pumps," Alec explained matter-of-factly. "These babies pull in air from outside, send it into levels above, return old air, and pump it back outside."

"I thought this was a waste plant?"

"Is. Waste air is waste too. I can show you the shit too, Mister, if that's your belly."

"Not really. Okay, so this is for all levels?"

"Naw, doubt it. I think up above 40 or 50 they pull from someplace else. I bet they get pure air there."

They walked past at least a dozen rows before coming to a large wall.

"Doesn't seem like that many," Talbot said.

"This is an outer room. Extends both ways around the entire level. How many machines we got here Jerome?"

"One hundred fifty-six thousand," Jerome said softly.

Talbot gave a low whistle, Alec beamed.

"You guys the only crew?" Talbot asked. He had not seen anyone else yet.

"Sure, Mister. Jerome and I keep up 156,000 machines. Naw, just fuckin' with ya. We never touch 'em. We just do vent checks for this area."

Ahead was a large door. Coming out of the wall above it were huge pipes.

"Intake valves," Alec said. "We'll go underneath. Wouldn't

want to be in there right now. They'd suck you into a fan mighty quick."

Alec opened the door and they climbed into a short hallway, the ceiling only about four feet tall that stretched into darkness. Alec tapped his wrist and small lights lit the way. They scooted along until they got to a small compartment.

"So yeah, the filters are in the tunnel above us. Normally we pull 'em, clean 'em off, and put 'em back. But we also give a look outside, just to make sure everything is okay. That's when we found her. There's an access hatch right here." Alec looked back at Talbot, his weasel smile in full bloom. "Ready, Mister?"

Talbot felt his stomach turn. He had never thought much about the outside. The city was outside to him. The parks, the streets were outside. Only if you tried very hard and thought about it did you realize that of course you weren't outside on the street but under a roof. And above that roof was another level, and above that, another level, and so on. Outside was a concept, not a place.

Alec tapped his wrist and the hatch gave a sudden jolt. A high whistling sound pierced the air.

"Wind," Alec shouted above the increasing noise.

He gave the door a gentle shove and it flew open, banging against the outside. Bright light, brighter than any light Talbot had ever seen, streamed in. It blinded him as he felt cold air rush over him, blowing him so hard he felt like falling backwards. He steadied himself and slowly made his way to the hatch. The light hurt his eyes as he reached the open doorway. Placing his hand on the wall he leaned out and quickly pulled himself back in. All he had seen was a dizzying blur of blue and white and a flash of green.

He felt sick and his legs were weak.

Alec was laughing, but Jerome put his hand on Talbot's arms to steady him.

"Pretty freaky, iddinit?" Alec yelled over the wind. "Look one more time mister, then we'll go."

Talbot swallowed hard and looked at Jerome, who nodded. So Talbot edged forward one more time and poked his head out, his grip tight on the frame of the hatch. He closed his eyes before leaning out and then holding his breath slowly opened them. The light remained blinding, but his eyes were adjusting to the bright glare. A dull blue sky dotted with clouds lay stretched before him, the sun behind a layer of haze but still bright. Gasping a breath and then holding it he looked down. Far below was land, brown mostly with patches of green stretching into the horizon. He stared at it for what felt like an eternity. Then Alec's voice broke his reverie.

"The ledge is above," he shouted.

Still gripping tightly Talbot craned his neck and saw a ledge directly overhead. It was narrow, not more than a couple of feet across. He moved his head out as far as he dared while still being able to keep his body inside. Just past the edge of the ledge he could see upward. A complex mass of brick and metal spiraled upwards into the clouds. The whole world began to spin. His stomach flipping violently he pulled himself back into the room and willed himself not to vomit. He bent over and by holding very still for what seemed like hours, he was able to stop the nausea.

Drenched in sweat he slowly straightened up. Alec was closing the hatch while Jerome kept a fearful eye on Talbot.

"You okay?" Alec asked airily as he checked that the hatch

was locked.

"Will be."

"You got it bad, but no worse than most. I knew you were gonna be in trouble when you looked up. Gets most people."

Talbot said nothing; he was concentrating on breathing.

"Seen enough, Mister?"

Talbot nodded.

The trip back was just as fast and reckless, but Talbot barely noticed. He was too focused on just trying to breathe. In a strange way the violence of Alec's driving helped take his mind off the feeling in his stomach. In what seemed like mere minutes they were back by the large, open area at the front of the building. Talbot got out of the truck but Alec and Jerome stayed in.

"Uh, look, thanks," Talbot said "If you think of anything else or remember anything from the girl let me know, okay?"

"Sure, Mister. Why you so damn interested in this girl anyway? Family?"

"No, but she may be connected to a girl that disappeared a few days ago."

Alec snorted. "People disappear every day, Mister, especially around here. Watch yourself."

Jerome, who had been silent the entire time since he had given the number of air machines suddenly blurted out, "It's dangerous. Don't."

"Shut up, Jerome. We don't owe him nothing," Alec hissed.

Before Talbot could ask Jerome what he meant Alec slammed the car forward down the hall. Talbot stood there a moment and then went through the doors into the open area. The young lady was gone, but a few more people milled about. A couple of them looked up as he walked through to the front door, but no one said anything.

This time coming out into the open street did not feel refreshing. The ceiling seemed to hover like a specter over the city. The air seemed stale again. He was mulling over and over again about the girl on the ledge. It hit him as he started up the street back to Market that he had forgotten to ask what CSA was.

He tapped his watch. "What do the letters CSA stand for?"

A small screen popped up with a long list of responses. There were at least a dozen organizations listed.

"Nice watch."

Talbot looked up. He had stopped in front of a long building without any noticeable door or entryway that made the block feel abandoned. There was no one on the street except for a very large man with a bald head who was a few inches taller than Talbot. Instinctively Talbot thrust his hand down, almost behind his back. Talbot put his head down and went to side-step the man. The man blocked him.

"I said, nice watch."

Talbot's stomach told him this was not going to end well.

"Give it to me," the man demanded.

Talbot's face stretched in shock. Everyone wore a watch. It was the device that did everything, from open doors to pay for meals and transport. No one stole watches; everyone had them.

Talbot glanced around; there was no one near. Suddenly the man grabbed Talbot's arm and wrenched it painfully at an angle.

Talbot fell to his knees grimacing.

"I told you to give it to me, shit. Gotta make it hard, huh?"

The man kicked Talbot in the stomach, sending him sprawling on the ground. Several more well placed kicks ended up in Talbot's face and sides. He saw several people on the other side of the street scurrying away. Soon a second figure appeared. Talbot hoped it was someone coming to help, but he knew better. The second man put his hand on the first man's chest.

"Easy, just the watch is all we want mister."

Talbot stared up but did not say anything. The second man took his hand away and nodded. The larger, first man aimed a kick at Talbot's chest. With a sickening crunch Talbot felt something snap. He hoped it was just his ribs. Pain shot through him. Shaking, he held out the arm with the watch on it. The second man roughly ripped it off and held it up.

"Nice one," he said. Then he dropped it on the ground and with a violent stomp, smashed the watch. Talbot watched, seething. They weren't even stealing it, they just wanted it destroyed.

"Grab him."

His body screaming in pain as they manhandled him, the two men dragged Talbot by his hands down the street, past the block-long building, and into what passed for an alley that was empty save a large shed. The men dragged him behind the shed.

The shorter man was slightly out of breath. He looked peeved. "Shoulda just given us the watch, asshole. Give him some souvenirs."

The larger man kicked Talbot a few more times, although it felt as if his heart was no longer in it. The second man must have sensed it too. With an expression of disgust he pushed the larger man aside and pulled a blackjack from his coat. The last thing Talbot remembered was seeing the black shape coming towards his head.

Talbot vaguely remembered coming to and crawling into the corner between the shed and building before passing back out. When he woke up again it was night, or at least what passed for night. The lights were low. He lay there for a long time, trying to feel which parts of his body were broken. It felt like his nose may have been broken and for sure at least a rib. He head was splitting but as he gingerly felt his skull he didn't think there was any damage up there.

It took a few minutes, but he was able to eventually stand up. He was pretty sure he looked a mess, but at least it was late. The streets might be empty and he could sneak back to the lift without much effort. But the Market's street was full of people. He must have looked a sight as people parted ways on the sidewalk as he made his way slowly back to the lift. His entire body was sore and his ribs shot white hot pain with every breath. He would have stopped at the Medrache saw, but without a watch he had no way to pay.

He sat down near the lift station and with much effort extracted the transit card from his pocket. He reflected on his watch. Talbot knew the attack had been no mere mugging. The two had expressly taken and then destroyed his watch. Watches were useless off the wrist of the registered person, but there was black-market for used watches that had been hacked. It might have brought a few credits. But they just smashed his. Without a watch in a place like level eight, or heck, any level, Talbot was essentially a dead man. He had no way to pay for food or shelter or, in his case, medical care. But most important of all he would not be able to access the lift. He could not make it back.

Whoever the two men were working for had rolled the dice. If they took away his means of leaving, chances were he would either be forced to stay on the level until he could contact help or, in the worst case scenario, work until he earned enough to get back. But as Talbot thought about, that was not the worst case. Worst case was that something happened to him, someone outright killed him or kidnapped him, sold him into labor on an even lower level. Human trafficking was difficult because of the metrics that tracked people, but it was not impossible. It happened all the time to people who lost all their money. He had effectively lost his money until he could get back to 29 and sort out a new watch.

He fingered the black transit card and reflected on it as the door to the lift opened for him. Geertz had given it to him just the day before, so Talbot doubted it was Treasure who had ordered the hit. Besides, it did not stink of a gang operation. He would be dead in that alley if it had been a gang. It had to be someone or some group who wanted him out of the picture. Talbot took cold comfort in knowing that he must be getting closer to finding out what was going on.

He just wished he knew what it was he now knew that had

gotten someone so scared.

Once in the lift he decided he would not go back to 29, but to 31, where, he hoped, Aria would be waiting. He could borrow credits from her to go to the Medrac, but then he had to fill her in about what he had learned. Maybe she knew what the CSA was. Then tomorrow he could go back down to 29 and get a new watch.

The clock on the lift said it was just about midnight. So much for going down for a few hours. As Talbot got off the lift he wondered if Aria was up, worried about him. A few minutes and a subway ride later he was at her building. He punched her number into the screen. It took a moment but a bleary eyed Aria greeted him. She visibly jumped when she saw him.

"Tal?"

"Lemme in, Aria."

"What happened?"

"Just buzz me in already."

The screen went blank and a second later the door clicked. Talbot felt a wave of relief wash over him. He headed for the elevator. On the way he passed a small mirror on the wall, artfully placed so people could check their state before going out, or heading up as the case may be. Talbot glanced and inwardly cringed. Both eyes were already purple, as was his nose, visibly swollen. His face was dirty and smeared with blood.

Aria open the door to the flat with tears in her eyes. "Tal, what happened? I knew eight was a bad idea."

"Yeah, well, I guess you were right. I got mugged, sort of."

"You look awful. You need to get to a Medrac; you shouldn't have come here first."

"Well, that's the rub, I had no choice." Talbot held up his bare wrist.

"They took your watch?"

"Yeah, so I hate to ask but—"

"Of course. Let me get some decent pants on. There's a tech not a block away." Aria went back to her bedroom, Talbot could hear the closet door open and close. "How the hell did you get back up?" she asked, her voice muffled as she pulled on a shirt.

"I have contacts, even down there." He said this almost automatically. He didn't want to go into Geertz now; it would feel like a betrayal to Aria, having kept it from her for so long.

Aria came out, dressed in black pants and a neon yellow top. "Lucky you."

"Hardly lucky. Ach!" Aria had gone to give Talbot a kiss, or a hug, he wasn't sure, but his ribs did not feel like anyone getting even close to him. "Ribs," he explained. Aria gasped appropriately.

Five minutes later Talbot felt immeasurably better as the Medrac automaton injected a painkiller into his arm. Unlike the hangover cure or the cold/virus booster shot, Talbot's injuries would not be entirely gone once he left the small booth.

A screen dropped down and a virtual face appeared, alarmingly asexual. "You have three broken ribs. Your nose is not broken but is bruised. You have multiple bruises. You appear to have suffered a concussion as well. Were you in a fight?"

"Sort of."

"Injuries of this nature must be reported to protocol. When did this occur?"

"I dunno…about noon?"

"What location?"

"Off Market Street, on level eight." Talbot smiled, in part because the painkiller was now giving him a warm feeling down to his toes but also because he knew the last little bit of information would short circuit the automaton. The face disappeared for a moment and then flickered back on.

"I'm sorry, that is out of jurisdiction. Protocol advises against travel to levels below number 11."

"I'll keep that in mind."

"You're injuries will have to heal on their own, I can prescribe painkillers and some pills to advance healing. Would you like me to do so?"

"Hell yes, please."

A moment later two vials of pills dropped into a bin on the wall. Then the screen flashed a credit amount. Aria held her wrist up to the screen, the balance went to zero and the door clicked open.

"Ever wonder what would happen if you didn't pay?" Aria asked casually.

"The door stays locked and the Medrac calls protocol," Talbot said as he tested his legs now that he could barely feel anything. Aria looked at him with some shock but then laughed.

"I keep forgetting you're a tough guy."

They went back to the flat and Aria grabbed two bottles of beer from the fridge and sat down with them next to Talbot.

"Thanks. And what are you drinking?" he joked, reaching for one of the bottles.

Aria rolled her eyes. "I guess you deserve both. I hope the trip was worth it."

Talbot took a long swig and then settled back into the couch. His body gave a dull ache, but the pills did their job pretty well. He sighed. "Well, yes and no."

"Tell me what you found."

"Not a lot really. Protocol is hiding behind 20 feet of concrete down there. But I did get to talk to the guys who found the girl. They think she fell."

"Fell? From some roof or something?"

"No, outside. From outside."

"That's impossible."

"No, no, it's not. I never thought about it, have you? About the outside, I mean. Aria, it's weird. So weird and scary as hell, but there is an outside."

"Well, yeah, of course."

"You ever seen it?"

Aria shrugged. "Why would I have?"

"It was weird. Anyway, they found her on a ledge, dead. Weird."

Aria laughed. "You need to expand your vocab, Tal."

"What? It was weird."

"That's it? You got nearly killed for that?"

"Well, more or less, yeah."

Talbot settled back into the couch. He wasn't sure why he was leaving out the bit about the jumpsuit and the CSA. He was remembering what Aria had said about talking before you knew everything. He wanted to find out what the hell the CSA was first. He felt as if he should know what it meant, and didn't want to seem any more foolish than he already felt.

"What about the watch?" Aria asked after some silence.

"I'll go down to 29 tomorrow and get a new one. I know a guy."

"I mean, what happened?"

"I was stupid, I guess. Wrong place, although…"

"What?"

"Well, it was strange."

"That you got mugged down there? You must have stood out pretty well."

"Sure, but at first they just asked for the watch, as if they were going to steal it."

"But it's biometric set."

"I know. But you know there are ways around that. But once they got it they just smashed it and then beat me up."

Aria looked concerned. "Do you think it was a set up?"

"Could be…yeah, pretty sure it was."

"Who knew you were going down there?"

"Besides you?"

Aria lightly punched him on the arm. He tried not to but he winced. "Oh sorry, sorry. Yes, besides me."

"Well…"

"What?"

"Okay, look don't get mad, but I thought I needed protection. I stopped by on 19."

"You what?"

"Relax, I—"

"Protection?" Aria stood up, anger rising in her face. "That nearly got you killed."

"I'm not sure they are who set me up."

"Who then?"

"Well, people down there were unfriendly from get-go: the protocol, the guys at the plant, heck it could have just been two guys."

Ari was pacing. "Come on, Tal, think about it. They meant to scare you or at least get you to leave."

"Leave? They knocked me out, left me for dead in an alley. But yeah, I think they meant to send a message. Wrong way."

"What?"

"Wrong way to send a message. Just makes me curiouser and curiouser, Aria."

"Make me nervous, Tal."

Aria sat down and took Talbot's face with her hands. "Look at me. You're too good, too smart, to get caught up in some rat snare. I know you want to help that girl, but it's been close to a week."

"Five days."

"And there is no sign of her. Plus now you almost got killed."

"What about Mill?"

"He's dead and there's no evidence he's connected with those girls beyond coincidence. Leave it before you accidentally cross something else. Look, I've got contacts with protocol up and down the levels. There's a detective opening on 36. I can get you in there, Tal. I know you'd do well and just think how much better things would be. And on 36 people actually like the protocol."

Tal laughed and shook his head, then gently took Aria's hand away. "Just give me a couple more days." He reached over and kissed her lips. She pushed back.

"Do you think you can just change the subject by kissing me?"

"Yes."

CHAPTER TWELVE

Talbot woke up mid-morning the next day still stiff and sore, but his head felt a lot better. He popped one of the pills and felt his ribs melt away. After a quick shower he headed for the lift to 29. There was a note from Aria on the screen by the door that left him wondering:

Tal, meeting tonight. See you tomorrow.

Back on 29 Talbot felt immeasurably better. He felt safe, comfortable, but not like going home to his parent's flat. If his mum saw the state he was in, he would never hear the end of it. He decided to see his friend, get a new watch, and then head back up to 31 and spend the night alone in Aria's apartment.

Talbot's friend owned an electronics store in a mini-mall off the main shopping road on 29. Talbot knew the guy might be able to help him with more than just the watch. The sign hanging over Kerr's Electro was spelled out in dancing nano lightbots that would occasionally rouse themselves to spell out various items offered with random offensive slang added periodically: Watches, Seeks, Cables, Witch-farts, Home Cook Boxes, Vid Screens.

Talbot was laughing when Kerr popped up from behind a

stack of boxes in the corner. He looked puzzled.

"The bots are going on about cook boxes again, Kerr."

"Hey!" Kerr gave the frame of the shop a sharp thump. The lights in the sign dissolved into a blur of color and then reformed into the words Piss Off before morphing into Kerr's Electro.

"What can I do you for, Tal? Hey, where's your watch?"

"You don't miss much do you?"

"Didja loose it?"

"Someone lost it for me down on eight."

"What the hell where you doing down there? I always said you were an idiot, but really, Tal."

"I was sight-seeing. Now can you set me up with a replacement or not?"

"Fifty credit."

"Fifty? When I upgraded last they were 30."

Kerr put both hands on the counter and sighed. "Tal, that was what, five years ago? Someone did you a favor to take that thing from you. Did it even tell time anymore?"

Talbot laughed, "No, but it worked fine."

Kerr smiled and began to dig through boxes behind him. "So, how's the love life, Tal? Still seeing that Jill woman?"

"Jill? Oh, God no."

"She was a handful. So who's the lucky gal now."

"No one."

"Not surprised. Girls like a guy who isn't six cycles behind with his watch."

"No one cares about that except for you. Besides, I guess I am seeing someone now, sort of."

Kerr put a box down on the counter and looked up. "Sort of? Tal, Tal, you've got it all wrong. That's not the way it works. Either you're in or you're not."

"Very funny. There's a detective in protocol, up some levels. Name's Olsen. She and I met on a case. Nothing more than psychical right now."

"The best kind, if you ask me."

"Kerr, when was the last time—"

"Got married two months ago."

"Oh hey, congratulations!"

"Thanks. See, if you'd come around more often…" Kerr opened a box and held up a black plastic bag, reading the label. He frowned and looked at Talbot. "You met a protocol from an upper level on a case down here?"

"Yeah. Mill, the jeweler?"

Kerr's face remained sober. "Never heard of him. What level is she from?"

"Thirty-four."

"Thirty-four down here? What was the deal?"

"Dunno. Gang hit, they think. Maybe not. I got ideas, which is what I wanted to talk to you about some."

"You're telling me a protocol detective comes down from 34 to 29 and you end up with a dunno case?" Kerr leaned in. "You can tell me man, what's up?"

Talbot was taken aback. He had gotten so close to the Mill case he didn't realize how odd it looked. "Kerr, I'm telling you I don't know. Guy got hit, Treasure left a card, except it wasn't really Treasure and then his granddaughter got snatched. So here I am."

"Sounds like a cluster fuck, Tal. Alarm bells going off left and right, man."

"Okay then, help me out."

"Whatcha got?"

"CSA."

"What's that?"

"I was hoping you could help me. There are plenty of things that correspond to those initials."

"So it's a thing, not a person?"

"Yeah. I was down on eight to follow up on a girl that had gone missing. They found her body on eight outside on a ledge."

Kerr gave a low whistle. "Okay, so what is CSA to it?"

"It was on her uniform."

Kerr walked over to a small keypad on the counter and typed in the acronym. "Dozens of hits, none very likely."

"I know. I did the basic search."

"How about for level eight?…Hmmm, nothing really good."

"No, wait! That's it—not level eight. Try 10."

"You said eight."

"I know, but she fell from 10."

"Fell? Wow, okay…Huh."

"What?"

"CSA might be Catalonia Spacefarers Association. She was in uniform, right?" Kerr swung the screen around and an instantly recognizable logo appeared.

"Okay…," Talbot said slowly. "What the hell is that then?"

"Spacefarers. Never heard of them?"

"No."

"Well, not just CSA. There are hundreds of them, mostly on lower levels or way, way up."

"What the hell are Spacefarers?"

"Uh, astronauts. Jeeze, Tal, I knew you were 29-focused, but come on."

"You mean like outer space?"

"Sure."

"So they like the space program and are fans of it or something?"

"Space program? Wow, Tal."

"What? Why do we have a space program? I thought that was useless, can't get from here to there fast enough."

"True, true, and every other planet outside our system is light years away, decades or more."

"Okay, so what are we doing?"

"Mining, mostly."

"Mining? On the moon or something?"

"That was the first. It was an easy one: a short distance, a few days away. Fuel, time is no problem. Here, try this one on."

Kerr handed Talbot a bulky silver-colored watch. Talbot eyed it suspiciously. "What, am I—a 15-year-old girl?" Kerr smirked and grabbed the watch back. "So there's the moon. Explain what the CSA does then."

"The moon is fine, but limited. It's small, weird gravity, limited resources. The moon tops out at about 10 thousand folks. There are better places to get stuff, better places to send people."

"Send people? I thought this was about mining?"

"Talbot, take a look around. Notice anything we got a lot of here, and anything else we are short of?"

"Uhm, obnoxious people who can't find me a decent watch?"

"Funny. Should make you go to the Townies and explain how you lost your watch. No—people and space. We got a lot of people and not much space. Can't build up forever, Tal."

"So, go out. I've seen out, Kerr. There's lots of it."

"Not really. Look, cities are the only safe space anymore. And it's the same all over: not enough space in the cities."

"What about down? Man, you should have seen eight: practically empty, Kerr."

"Really, no shit? You wanna stay down there, set up a mansion? Stretch your legs?"

"Okay, okay, so no one wants to live down there. Spruce it up, I dunno. Or just build up. Everyone's in such a goddamn hurry to get up a level anyway."

"Easy, I'm on your side, amigo. That's the issue: they've been building up forever, man. But there is a limit. There are already problems on the lowest levels. Population, man, is always the problem."

"So build a new city."

"Sure, but where? Too many already, Tal," Kerr said from behind a pile of boxes in the corner. "The answer," he said, pulling out a jet black box from the pile, "is space. Ship people off."

"But the moon's full up or something, right?"

"Right."

"So where then? Mars?"

"Mars and Europa. Mars to live, Europa to mine. They have a space station above it. From there, work the solar system."

"But, isn't Mars like months away?"

"Three or four, but that's not the bad part." Kerr set the black box down. "It's a one-way ticket. Fuel takes up too much room. They need to send supplies and stuff. They've been going now for 10 years, but they still don't have the capacity to be self-sustaining. So if you go, you don't come back."

"Really?"

"Really—at least not now. Maybe in 30–40 years they might have return trips. It's a long-term thing…really long term. They use the materials they mine to build new stuff, new parts of the mining operation. But the idea is that in say 20 years they'll start sending material back; in 40 years people—if they can come back. Most will be dead probably, or weak from reduced gravity, who knows what else."

Talbot was silent for a moment. Kerr studied him. "Pretty weird, huh? They don't talk much about it in the media. Political implications—people might panic about the structure of the city. But it's tied up lots of long-term capital; there's plenty of big time money in it. Here, try this."

Kerr handed Talbot a sleek, low profile matte black watch. Talbot played with it in his hands for a moment and then slid it on.

Kerr laughed. "The expression on your face. That one's 70, by the way."

"What? You said 50!"

"For your basic model. This one's special, Talbot—designer."

Talbot eyed it, a miserable expression on his face. "Fuck you, Kerr. This one is nice, but I can't afford it."

"Forty today, 30 next week."

Talbot sighed and nodded. He stroked the watch and a light blue screen floated in the air. Kerr entered a code and Talbot felt the watch buzz slightly as it downloaded his metrics.

"I've pulled your old stuff, canceled your old phone, so most of your stuff should be in the new watch."

"Okay, thanks. So, still not sure where something like this CSA comes in," Talbot said, still staring at the watch.

"That's one of the stickier points. Big money can tie up capital for a few decades. Risky but possible. The real problem is essentially killing off people."

"What?!" Talbot looked up, momentarily forgetting about the watch.

"Metaphorically speaking. Well, maybe not. It's like a death sentence, no? Here, get on board this spacecraft, take a really risky voyage for three months, and get to a place that makes level eight look like a luxury resort. And you can never come back. Sound like fun?"

"Well, okay, maybe not to you and me, but if you're stuck down someplace, that might seem like a good deal. A decent job, bet you can send pay home, you get out from under."

"Yeah, sure, and it is. Trust me: if you'd asked anyone on eight about CSA they'd shove you out of the way to get on board. But it doesn't work that way. There's a limit as to who they want going. You have to be pretty smart, healthy—attributes that people down below are short of. Hell, most people on this level wouldn't qualify."

"So what does CSA have to do with this?"

"So the government needed some help getting people to go. They offered—still offer—a reward for those who volunteer. I think they call it a signing bonus; a bounty is too crass. So these for-profit orgs sprang up looking for people who want to go. Well, more like convince people to go."

"But you said they want upper level people; this CSA is on 10."

"Ten is a launching area. The proper headquarters for CSA is probably higher up—40s or 50s even. I can do some research."

"That high? Why bother? The cost of doing business up there…"

"They get a cut of the bounty. It's an okay business, not a great one. Most of these outfits are lucky if they send three or four people a year. Here, I'll show you. CSA here only sent…holy flurkin snit! They've sent 15 people in the past three years."

Talbot felt his neck hairs stiffen. "About a dozen women, right."

Kerr looked up and nodded, wide eyed. "Tal, what the fuck is this? You are not telling me stuff."

"Like I said, I don't know exactly, but I think it's some pretty bad stuff the case is moving towards. In the past couple of years about a dozen girls have gone missing at Atlanta on 31, each time Mill was on that level around that time."

"You think—?"

"I have no idea. Nothing connects Mill except the coincidence of being on the level at the same time."

"You said his granddaughter went missing after he died."

"Yes," Talbot rubbed his face. "That's part of the problem. Nothing makes sense or fits nicely, but there is something here. And now this…"

Kerr's face was pale. "Talbot, I'm telling you: if there is some connection with CSA and Mill and the girls, it's worse than bad." His voice was a whisper. "The money involved, the people, it's all higher level stuff—stuff that will melt you, Tal."

"Yeah, I know. Look, Kerr, don't do anything else, okay? I mean, stay sterile, ya know? If anyone asks, tell 'em we talked about girls or something—you know, lady trouble."

Kerr laughed. "Yeah, sure, Tal. Enjoy the watch, bud."

But as Talbot walked away, he saw Kerr's face etched in worry.

Talbot spent the afternoon walking the streets of 29 aimlessly. He used the time to turn the facts over in his head and try to make some sense of them. His first thought was that this CSA outfit was snatching girls and sending them to Mars, but a quick review of the whole thing laid that to rest. Candidates who joined up through one of these organizations or even just walked in the door underwent plenty of scrutiny. At the very least the girl's metrics would have shown up. And there would have been hours of interviews and tests—at any point the girls would have plenty of opportunity to protest.

It would have almost been nice to at least know the girls were still alive and stranded someplace on Mars or around Europa, but Talbot thought that highly unlikely. The more he thought about it more, the more he wondered if the whole CSA thing was a red herring. Perhaps the girl had escaped from Mill or whoever and somehow found her way into a lunch pad, grabbed clothes, and then either accidently fell or jumped on purpose, trying to escape recapture. If it was anything like eight, 10 might be an ideal place to bring a victim for whatever Mill might have done to them.

As the day got late Talbot was getting beyond tired. His ribs were aching, despite downing several more pills. He needed a place to rest and to quiet his spinning head. If he headed back to his parents' flat he would get neither. He made his way over to the lift and headed for 31.He let himself in to Aria's apartment with his new watch. It did bother Talbot a little that it was so easy to pull material off a dead and smashed watch, but he knew most of what he considered to be on his watch was really on an electronic cloud someplace. Still.

Once inside he did not even bother getting undressed, He crashed onto the bed in the guestroom and passed out.

He woke to feel his wrist buzzing. Someone was calling him. He glanced outside; it was night. He looked at the watch, it was 2:00 a.m. He had been asleep for 10 hours. A screen popped up and Kerr's face filled it.

"Sorry, were you asleep?" Kerr seemed nervous, jittery.

"It's 2:00 a.m. I have three cracked ribs. Yes, I was asleep."

"Listen, can't talk long. Randomizer won't stay random forever. I did some research on our friendly spacefarers."

"Yeah?' Talbot yawned, rubbed his eyes.

"Incorporation docs. Don't worry, I did it all backways so no tracing, but get a load of this: the firm is incorporated on 45 and guess who's name is all over them?"

"Hmm?" Talbot said.

"One Aria Olsen. Crossed her and she's a detective—but you know that, don't you? She has a 49 percent share in CSA and is in league with people on 45, lover boy. Where are you?"

Talbot felt every cell in his body scream awake. "Don't call back, Kerr. I may need you again if I get out of this alive, okay?"

"It's randomized."

"Promise."

"Okay, jeesh. Bye."

The screen vanished and Talbot found himself alone in the dark.

CHAPTER THIRTEEN

Talbots first impulse was to flee as fast as possible, but he wasn't sure where he would go or what he would do, exactly. He figured the best bet was to wait in the flat for Aria to show up. He could ask her about CSA. It could be a coincidence.

The trouble was, the coincidences were beginning to pile up.

He set about doing what he termed a light search. He had learned this trick from his mentor. No sense in overturning the place; that was drama for the telenovelas. He went around the flat opening drawers, pulling out books…so many books. But the place was clean, really clean. Maybe it even had been cleaned. Talbot wondered for a moment if the place was really connected to Aria at all.

Morning came and he carefully made sure the apartment looked as it had before the search. Then he remembered the picture frames. They had always been turned off, but he wondered if they had anything on them.

He found one on a shelf and slid the switch. It flickered to life. A series of images played across the screen, slowly dissolving into one another. Aria through the years with her dad, both aging rapidly as the pictures scrolled across. No sign of a mother. Aria looked nothing like her father. He seemed soft around the edges, always rumpled. She always stood ramrod straight, a look of fierce determination on her face.

Talbot switched the frame off and looked around. Another, smaller frame was near the kitchen counter. He idly switched it on next. A few shots of Aria and her dad again, then some of Aria and what looked like people from work, some of her on vacation, in a nice hotel with random people he assumed were friends—and then her next to a man with white hair, cleanly shaved on one side.

Talbot nearly dropped the frame. He picked it up and studied the photo. The man was clearly older, and his hair was not shaved—the side of his head was scarred no hair grew there. It seemed pretty clear that was the man that Deesee had told him about. He broke out into a sweat and his hands shook as panic rose up in him. Things were falling into place but he still wasn't sure how they exactly fit together.

Everything was connected but to what and where? Kerr had told him that CSA was headquartered on 45, so the threads must at least lead up to that level, if not higher. Somehow CSA must be trafficking the girls, but Talbot could not figure out how or why.

Suddenly the door to the flat swished open. Aria walked in and found Talbot standing at the kitchen counter where the frame was still on, brightly scrolling.

"Aria," Talbot said, in what he hoped was a neutral tone. His mind was racing. He saw her glance to the counter then back to him. The hard look from the photos come over her face. She walked over and sat down in the big leather easy chair. Talbot stood there, uncertain what to do.

"I got the alarm yesterday afternoon, but I figured it was you. You get some rest?"

"Yes, I did." Talbot said, still standing as if afraid to move.

She cocked her head and looked back at the counter. "Old pictures, people I used to know." She stood back up and came over to stand right in front of Talbot, still frozen. He watched her warily. "What's up, Tal?" she asked, her voice level but cold. "You look like you've seen a ghost."

"No, not a ghost. What's going on, Aria?"

She smiled, but her eyes never warmed up. "Your friend with the phone call...pretty clever, huh?" Talbot closed his eyes and swore to himself. "He was clever, you know. We can't trace where it came from. He Treasure? No matter, I heard what he told you. I would have come sooner Tal, but I had...things to do." Aria circled around him. "Tal, Tal, Tal...you should have listened to me. I really could have gotten you a job up on 36."

"You going to tell me what's going on?"

"No," she said, her voice cracking some. "No."

"So you murdered Mill. then?"

"Of course not, Tal. Give me some credit. No, that one is the real mystery. It's an unfortunate one. Not for Mr. Mill. He was already dead, he just didn't know it. But unfortunate for those left behind—you, me, others. His death was not part of the plan...well, not that soon anyway. You cannot imagine the problems his death has caused."

"Okay, so what about the CSA?"

"Don't ask, Tal. It's better that way." Her voice was hard but

Talbot thought he could see light in her eyes.

"So, all this?" Talbot gestured around the room. "Is it real at least?"

Aria sighed. "Yeah, a little souvenir from dear old dad, like I said."

"Whatever you've gotten caught up in Aria, we can undo."

"Caught up in, like I'm twelve? Please," she laughed. "I'm not caught up in anything, Tal. I'm running the shit, baby!" Aria rummaged around the kitchen and pulled out a tall, blue bottle of synthine. She unscrewed the top, pulled a long draught, and sat back down in the easy chair. Talbot still did not move.

"Tal, look at me—really look at me. Wanna know who I am, who I really am?"

"Yes, I do Aria. I actually do," he said quietly.

"Look at me, I did good, no? I work on level 34, buddy…level 34. Not bad, huh?"

"No, not bad."

"It's fuckin great, Tal!" her voice loose as the synthine worked its magic. "Eleven levels since I was 15."

"Eleven? But—"

"Eleven! Dear old Dad raised me on 23 until he got a position on 31. I was sooo happy, but he just stopped there. He was happy on 31. Satisfied on 31. Satisfied stuck here. He got offers, Tal, offers from unis on 37, 42…even 45." She counted out the levels on her fingers. "Did he go? No! The idiot was so fucking stunned he got from 23 to 31 he froze up. Can you imagine if he had gone to 45? Look what I did from 31. People think Atlanta is hot shit, but it's not, Tal. It just isn't. All I could manage was 34. Thirty fuckin four.

People from 45…people from there, they go places. The average jump is 10 levels from 45. Can you imagine? Average jump from 31? One level, one fucking level."

"You beat that average, Aria. That's pretty good."

"But still fuckin lame, Tal. Think I'm happy stuck on 34 Tal?"

"No, I don't think you are."

"Damn right."

"Why not take the job on 36 then?"

"Oh no, baby, 36 is chump change. How about 45? That grab you?"

"That would be pretty amazing."

"Fuck, Tal! Just like Dad, so fucking limited. Level 45? Please, that's just the base point. Sky's the limit when you jump on the right lift, eh?"

"So you killed a dozen people just to get on the right lift?"

"Killed? Please, no one's been killed, dear Tal. Well, no one except for poor old Mr. Mill, the greasy pervert. And his granddaughter, who the fuck knows? No, everyone is happy, Tal. I made sure of that. Fucking happy as shit. Everyone except for me. But now, thanks to you, that's done. Time to move forward, cash in, and move up, baby. Too bad you won't come along."

Aria stood up, her eyes filled with tears, her face suddenly weary. Then it hardened again. "Fuck, Tal, I almost fell for your stupid ass. Now…now," she stopped and stood there.

"Aria, let me help you. We can fix this all."

"You still don't get it—there is nothing to fix. I'm not in trouble. It's the opposite of trouble. No one's in trouble…well, except for you." She stood up and came up to him, close. "There's still time,

Tal. Let me help you. I know a guy who can help. Afterward you'll be happy and we can go up together. You're a real asset, Tal, for the right people and with the right attitude."

Talbot's mind was on overdrive, I know a guy who can help. Afterward you'll be happy…What the hell was she going on about? Aria's clumsy attempt to kiss him brought him back to the present.

He gently pushed her away. "I think I need to leave now, Aria. I'm not sure what's going on, I really have no idea. Whatever it is that you're up to, I don't know what to say. If I had any real idea I would go to the protocol right away, but I honestly don't. So maybe we can just call it a draw, okay?" Talbot knew he was talking nonsense, except that most of it was true.

"Don't go Tal. Stay."

"I can't stay." Talbot walked towards the door but Aria did not move. She stared down at the floor, the half empty bottle of sythine in one hand.

"Goodbye, Tal," she whispered.

Talbot edged to the door, but she made no move. As quietly as he could he pulled the door open and stepped into the hallway. As the door clicked shut he felt waves of relief wash over him. He wasn't entirely sure what do to next, but he figured his next move was to get down to 19 as soon as he could. Maybe Geertz would let him hide out for a while until things cooled or he could figure this all out.

As fast as he could, he made his way down to the lift station. The streets were already filling up with people. Talbot marveled at how calm and easygoing they seemed, unaware as to what was going on around them. He had been unaware, taking for granted the world in which he lived. Now, he saw as if with new eyes. He saw the dirt, the wear, the suffocating space around them. They were just animals caged and waiting to be killed—for what, exactly?

The lift going down was crowded as commuters jostled to get on board. Talbot found himself being pushed back and decided to wait for the next lift. The area in front of the lift doors suddenly emptied after the doors closed and elevator slowly descended.

Talbot wasn't sure why he turned around; he must have sensed something. When he turned he saw a man in a grey suit with a shock of white hair and a shaved side of his head. The man was very purposely walking towards him. Talbot might have waited to see what the man wanted, except that he saw the man reach into the suit jacket front and pull out a taser.

Talbot broke into a run and without looking back could hear the man running behind him. The platform area was small, most of it taken up by the large lift area, which was closed off by a chest-high glass wall and the main exit to the street was on the other side of the lift. Talbot raced around the enclosure looking for an alternative exit. He could hear the man gaining on him. He began to panic, not sure if he could make it all the way around the large circle and out before the man got close enough to tase him.

He could see a few people filing onto the platform where the doors to the lift opened. He was too far away and wasn't going to make it. He glanced back and the man was only yards behind him. Talbot hesitated only a moment and then threw himself on the floor and felt a surge of electricity fly over his head.

The man had fired and missed. Talbot scrambled up as the man swore. He only had a few seconds before the taser recharged and the man could shoot again, this time from just a few feet away.

On pure instinct Talbot grabbed the top of the glass enclosure and jumped over it into the lift area. Only a very narrow, six-inch concrete ledge kept him from falling into what was essentially an open pit. Talbot looked down and felt that same sick feeling rise up as when he had been outside. The lift pit extended down seemingly forever. He looked back and the man with the white hair was raising the taser. Lights were flashing and bells going off. A loud voice boomed: Clear the area, clear the area.

Talbot realized that he had not just tripped an alarm, but the actual lift was coming down from above—fast. He looked back and the man now had the Taser aimed. Talbot glanced down the shaft and briefly wished he was anywhere else. He got to the edge, feeling the air pushing down. He jumped as the electricity passed above him again and heard the rushing roar of the lift coming down.

Talbot pressed himself against one of the many doorways set just under the rim of the lift platform in the lift shaft. He felt a terrible pull as the lift itself came down the shaft, the vacuum violently trying to suck him out. Seconds later it was over. The bottom of the lift had settled behind him, giving him very little room to maneuver. He felt for a latch on the door and pulled, the door gently opened inward. The door had a helpful message on it: open in case of emergency.

He stepped into the dark access hallway for a moment and could hear commotion above. Feeling suddenly faint, Talbot sat down, his chest pounding, and his ribs aching. He tried to collect his thoughts. He had to get away to some place, but where? How?

He got up and looked out the door. There was a few inches

between the lift body and the tunnel. He looked at the lift. It seemed to travel along a sort of vertical rail system up and down. As he looked down he saw the shaft extending into what seemed like infinity. He sighed. He knew what he had to do and it pained him as much as anything. He carefully took his watch off, aimed, and tossed it down the shaft.

"Fuck, 70 credits," he said mournfully as the watch tumbled down the shaft out of sight. He closed the door and waited.

The lift did not move. He could imagine the irate people on the platform, but what could he do? In a way, the whole thing was a real gift. As far as the man with the white hair was concerned, Talbot had jumped to his death and his metric would blink off the system when the watch smashed into the ground however many stories below. Talbot was officially dead and it felt surprisingly good.

The lift beside him began to work again after about 45 minutes. He sat there, waiting, listening to the lifts going by. He was itchy to get going, but didn't want to risk being seen. Finally after waiting another hour he felt safe enough to leave the compartment and carefully made his way through a series of small crawl spaces until he found a hallway. He was taking a chance, but he had to get out somehow. He hoped that either the hallway was not monitored, or if it was no one would care. He dropped down from a hatch about three feet off the ground and looked up and down the hallway. There were no visible cameras.

He made his way down until he got to a larger hallway, this time with plenty of cameras, but also people going up and down. He waited until he saw a small knot of three people and he casually fell in step behind them. He wasn't sure if someone was watching that they wouldn't immediately see him out of place, but it was a chance he had to take.

It took a few more minutes, but he was finally able to leave the hallway system and step back into the street. It took him a moment to realize he was some 12 blocks from the lift station. He formulated a new plan: he was not going to go to 19. Instead he headed back to Aria's flat.

He hung back from the building and found a spot to watch the front door beside a food cart. He had a hunch that once she found out he was dead, she would leave, and he had a pretty good idea where she would be headed. He just hoped he hadn't already missed her. To his relief he saw her familiar figure leave the building late in the afternoon. She did not even glance around so Talbot assumed word of his death had made it back to her. He trailed at her at a distance. He was used to this part, having often tracked people down or followed them, albeit usually for tawdrier affairs.

As Talbot suspected, Aria headed to the lift for 45. With him dead and Mill and Jahn also out of the picture, he figured Aria would want to wrap things up and go to her contact on 45. Or was it a partner, something more? He was eager to find out.

The lift was large and early evening full. This worked to Talbot's advantage as he paid with his card and squeezed on at the last minute. He had lost sight of Aria but the lift was finite so he was not worried.

A few minutes later the crowd in the lift spilled out onto the platform at 45. The lights outside flickered down a notch as the evening cycle come on. The station was crowded as several lifts emptied at the same time. It took him a moment to pick out Aria's black hair walking down the street.

To his surprise she walked past the business area adjacent to the station and continued on to a residential area. Talbot barely had time to take in his surroundings on 45, determined not to lose Aria. The ceiling was higher than 34; he estimated it ran more than 10 stories tall. The buildings were markedly newer, more modern, and more severe. The people dressed better on the streets. Talbot felt conspicuously shabby. Even Aria seemed dressed down.

After a few blocks the buildings became smaller and more spaced out. Talbot marveled at the use of space. Small buildings set into lots slightly larger than the building. Around each of the buildings, which were often only three or four stories tall, were gardens. Little trees, bushes with flowers, and even patches of neat green plants cut short were displayed in front of the buildings.

Finally, after several more blocks Aria stopped in front of a simple yet clearly elegant building only three stories tall. It appeared to be set into a double lot as the house only took up half the space. The rest of the property was manicured into a beautiful display of plants and flowers. Talbot wanted to simply stand there and stare. But Aria had already made it to the front doorway of the building and was talking to a small drop down screen. Seconds later the door opened and she vanished inside.

Talbot was not sure what to do next. He had a vague notion that he was going to follow Aria into an apartment flat or an office building and then sneak around until he could find a way to either see or overhear who she was meeting with. But this set up was like nothing he had ever seen. The building was small, meaning it probably did not have extensive duct work or maintenance tunnels. However, on the plus side he figured he would be able to walk around it and perhaps see through the windows.

He carefully crossed the street and began to circle the huge lot. Talbot assumed narrow allies, which separated the building from neighboring lots on either side, would enable him to make his way along the building without being seen. But as he edged to the left of the building, he saw there was a row of tall plants that separated the lot from the alley. The intent was privacy and prevented Talbot from seeing anything. His only option was to scale the fence that ran the perimeter of the lot. He figured there was a good chance the lot was alarmed but he would have to take that chance.

He reached out and carefully put a hand on the fence. Nothing happened. Could be a silent, he thought, but they weren't much of a deterrent. He hoisted himself over the fence and flopped down on the other side into dirt. Whoever owned the building had gone all out on the landscaping.

Still hearing no alarm, he carefully walked through the dirt and plants until he could see the building. Through the tall plants he saw that the building had large glass windows that ran the length and height of all three stories. On the bottom floor the windows were open. They appeared to slide into each other, nesting at the end. The effect was a room that bled into the outside of the house into the garden. Why not? thought Talbot. It wasn't as if the weather would be a cause for worry. And the plants hid the first floor from the neighbors well enough.

The room that ran down the side of the building and around back was large and almost empty. Great canvases hung on the interior wall and there were a few scattered couches and side tables. Sitting at the edge of one couch was Aria, looking nervous and somewhat small.

Talbot and Aria waited for several minutes—he in the garden, she on the couch—within a few feet of one another. Talbot was hidden by a large splay of leafy green plants in a huge container the size of Talbot's parents' flat back on 29.

After about 20 minutes a neatly dressed, somewhat older man came into the room. Aria bounded up and they embraced, kissing deeply. He was thin, tall, and classically handsome with high cheekbones and a sallow complexion. His hair was grey but kept short. He wore small-framed black glasses that seemed like affection to Talbot—most people just got their eyes fixed. Still, the man evoked a quiet power and authority. After their embrace Aria sat back down, her eyes focused on the man as if she did not want to miss a single word.

Talbot didn't either. He edged as close as he could.

"So, tell me Aria, how is the mess on 29?" The man busied himself pouring a glass of something amber.

"That's why I'm here. I think it is cleaned up."

"Think?" The man turned.

"Know. I know. Mantuk killed Talbot, so he's out of the picture."

"And the others?"

"Dealt with. Those on eight are bought off."

"Not good enough, Aria dear. I will handle them. You are too soft sometimes."

"I just felt there was no need."

"There is no need for loose ends. This whole thing was going fine, it has opened so many doors for me."

"For us."

"Yes, of course, dear, for us. People up top liked the results CSA was getting. I'm close, Aria. Within the next few weeks the mayor will appoint a new board and I'm all but guaranteed a seat. Level 65 Aria, can you imagine?" he mused, a serene, faraway smile on his face.

"Yes," she said simply, not smiling.

"Mr. Mill almost tripped us up. Unfortunate, so unfortunate. He was valuable, but of course nearing the end of his use. Any trace of the girl?"

"No."

"That is too bad. We'll have to keep on that as we can. No loose ends, Aria."

"Yes, of course."

Even hiding in the plants Talbot sensed there was an uneasy silence in the air.

"Did you clean out your stuff on 31 and 34 as we discussed?"

"Yes," Aria's face brightened. She looked up at the man. "It's all gone. Sterile. All I have to do is get my metrics back from 34."

"I can do that first thing tomorrow. Well done. Well done. Give me your watch then. You won't need that anymore; we'll set you up with a nice new one tomorrow."

Aria hesitated for a moment but then slipped off the watch

and handed it to the man.

"Have you found a place on 65 yet?" she asked lightly, trying to sound unconcerned.

"Yes. It is somewhat smaller than this, but no matter. I'm sure I will be able to afford bigger soon enough."

"I didn't take anything with me, like you asked. It's all been destroyed so I'll need to get some new clothes."

"Yes, of course," the man waved his hand dismissively.

"I thought tomorrow I could...," she looked confused at the expression on the man's face. "Or not..."

"Aria. My dear, dear Aria," he said without a trace of warmth.

Talbot felt himself go cold. Aria also sensed a change in the weather.

"I could not have done any of this without you, you know that?" Aria nodded, unsure where this conversation was going. "Yes, you were so key in finding Mr. Mill and the others to help us with the girls. Without you the CSA would have never caught the eye of those up top. I'm so grateful to you, Aria, for all of your help."

"I did it for us, Ludwig."

"Yes, I'm sure you did, dear. But of course there is no us." Aria froze, her face a mask. "I'm destined for great things, you and I both know that. And I simply cannot get there with some lower level...climber on my arm. Surely you realize that."

Aria did not move, her face remained passive, processing her world falling apart.

"I'm not evil, Aria. I respect the work you have done, I respect your drive. But now that most of the ends have been tied up, there is only one end left. You. Do not worry dear, you will not meet the same fate as others we dealt with. No, I think for you a much better fate awaits. Since you have so nicely erased your former life for me, I will help you begin anew. Dr. Roberts will be by tonight to…ease your mind."

Aria stood up, finally able to move.

"Sit down, dear," the man said coldly. He pulled her watch out of his pocket and dropped it on the floor. He stomped hard on it with a savage twist, shattering it. "Sit down! You can't get anywhere now anyway. Stop crying about it."

Tears were streaming down Aria's face, but other than that she showed no emotion. She stood there, in front of him. A minute ticked by and finally she spoke. "You know I will never go down willingly, Ludwig."

"The doctor."

Aria shook her head. "No, Ludwig, you know that isn't going to happen. I know you know this."

"Now, Aria, think about this, will you? I'm offering you a way out, a new start."

Aria smiled. "A new start?" she purred. Sounding more dangerous by the second. "A new start? Isn't that what you promised me before…dear. A new life on 65, more power and wealth than anyone on 23 had ever dreamed of. Imagine it? Yes, of course I did. Me, little me, rising up 42 levels. That's something that has to be admired. Even a climber like me has to admit it was too good to turn down; I was just blind to the fact that it was too good to be true."

She walked beside the man, who stepped back a step, to keep his distance. She fingered the bottle of amber liquid. "Go ahead,

Ludwig, do it. Do it now. Kill me. Don't let some fool down below do your dirty work!" anger in her voice for the first time.

"Aria, dear, I have no intention of killing."

"No? Really?" She screamed, "Come on, Ludwig, be a real man for once and do your own work!" Aria circled back around Ludwig, who was now standing very still. "Come on," she whispered. Ludwig stood there, barely breathing. "You're nothing but shit."

"Be reasonable, Aria. I've already called people to come, you won't get far."

"Give me a break. Even on 45 the protocol will take forever, Ludwig. I'm gonna cut you to pieces."

"I didn't call protocol," Ludwig said calmly.

Aria stopped pacing and stared at him. "I know you didn't call him; you're too little a man to."

"Stick around and see, Aria. Either way, it's too late. I can still convince him to let you stay below, but if you run now..."

Both of them were standing motionless when in a fluid motion Aria reached behind her back. There was flash of silver and then Aria was holding Ludwig up as he gasped for breath. She pushed him back and withdrew a long, silver blade. Then she stabbed him again, directly in the chest, a bloom of red forming on his shirt.

"Too late for you," Aria said softly as he crumpled to the ground.

Talbot stepped back deeper under the plants, his mind racing. Part of him wanted to leap out and offer Aria help. He could ask Geertz, get her to safety. But another part of him, a much louder part, was demanding he run. He had just watched Aria kill a man in cold blood—not with a gun or a taser, but a knife. Whatever he may have felt for Aria, he knew it was time to leave—and quickly.

But he lingered a moment and watched Aria. With a curiously blank expression on her face, she carefully stepped over the body and grabbed the amber liquid, which she downed in one long swig. She then let the room.

Talbot waited until she left and then ran as fast as he could to the fence. He pulled himself over and began to run as fast as he could back to the lift station. Whatever was going to happen, whoever the man had called, he did not want to be anywhere on 45 when those people showed up.

He kept to side streets and alleys, getting confused twice, before he saw the lift station lights illuminating the artificial night. Waiting for the lift down his mind was a blur. He needed time to think, time to process what was going on. Yet he had no idea where to go, exactly. He figured 29 was the best bet. He would be able to spend the night there at least; he would just have to deal with his parents. Then he could go back to Kerr and get yet another watch the next day. Then he would try and sort things out, maybe even pay Geertz a visit.

When the lift finally arrived and emptied, Talbot stepped inside. He was not surprised to see that he was the only one going down at this time of night, commuters and day workers having already come and gone. A few silent minutes passed as the lift waited for stragglers. Then he heard it: shouting voices coming up the platform.

He looked and saw her running as fast as she could. A melodic voice overhead warned the doors were about to close as she got closer and closer. The glass doors slid shut silently as Aria made it to the edge of the platform. She banged on the doors of the glass enclosure but the automated system was uncaring. For a moment the lift hung suspended as the same robotic voice warned her to stand back and wait for the next lift. Behind her three large men were running up, two with guns drawn.

She caught sight of Talbot, who stood in the middle of the over-lit, empty lift, staring at her. She was screaming, begging for help, crying—then her body jerked and a hole appeared in her shoulder, her ear disappeared in a spray of red. Then her face went abruptly blank, mouth open mid-scream, a red rose growing on her chest. As she crumpled to the ground the lift began its descent.

It was free to go down.

CHAPTER FOURTEEN

Instead of waiting for 29, Talbot slipped off at 32 as a small party of people sloshed their way on. If someone wanted to, they could track him through video, but that would not be their first choice; they would try metric first, so he had an advantage. The three men must have seen him on the lift. Even if they didn't connect him to Aria, they would see him as a witness to a killing, a loose end.

He walked half-way across 32, got in another lift, and went back up, this time to 37. He repeated his evasive action all night, partially to shake anyone who might still be trying to follow him, but also because he did not want to go back to his parents' flat.

Talbot jerked awake as the lift he was on stopped. He looked out, bleary-eyed, and saw he was on level 17. Random. He hopped out and looked for a clock. He finally found the time on a video commercial screen: 7:00 a.m. It was too early by a couple of hours to see Kerr, but Talbot was exhausted and hungry so he headed back and camped out in front of Kerr's Mall.

Kerr was early, the first to arrive. He did not seem surprised to see Talbot slumped over and asleep by the entrance. He gave him a kick and laughed when Talbot sputtered awake.

"Figured I'd see you this morning, or never again. Heard about your death. My condolences."

"So it's official?"

"Well, not so much, but in back channels, yeah. Your parents don't know you died. Yet. Protocol waits 48 hours to notify kin."

"I guess I should call them, but...," he held up his empty wrist.

Kerr smiled wryly. "Same?"

Talbot nodded.

Ten minutes later Talbot slipped the new watch on his wrist while he munched on a not-all-that-stale C-biscuit. Kerr pestered him with questions about what had happened.

"So, what's next?" he asked after Talbot described what he had seen.

"Going to 19 to see someone, then to 10. I want to talk to the launch folks down there."

"Here," Kerr tapped the floating screen towards Talbot's watch. "The address for the people who process CSA folks. They work with about four hundred different outfits, so be specific when you try and talk to them."

"How many damn things like CSA are there?"

"Tal, they have 46,000 people on Europa's platform alone; they aren't running the show with a dozen coeds."

"Not funny."

"Sorry, you're right. There are hundreds, maybe a couple of thousand. But I think most are legit; they're not kidnapping girls. Did you figure out how they do it yet? I mean, get past the screeners?"

"No. I think they do something with the metrics. Can you wipe someone's mind?"

"Sure, if you want a veggie afterwards. Really difficult to clean someone and reset them. People are not computers, as my wife often reminds me."

"Okay, so now I just have to find a place to crash. Can't go back to the folks'. Is there a podtel near here?"

"I have something better. I call it the naptel."

Kerr grinned and motioned Talbot to come behind the counter. Talbot rolled his eyes but followed. At the very back of the small shop was a wall of cabinets. Those underneath were accessed via a sliding door. Except instead of electronics, the space held a narrow mattress and a pillow.

"A hidey hole. For naps. Really," Kerr said, somewhat defensively.

"Yes, I see that. Little narrow for much else, dude. Thanks."

Talbot woke up hours later, disoriented. It took him a minute to remember where he was. He carefully slid open the door and peeked out. Everything seemed normal enough. Kerr turned around and smiled.

"Sleepy little bastard. It's an hour past my closing time. The wife will think I'm having an affair."

Talbot looked at his watch; it was six in the evening. He

wondered if Geertz kept regular hours but decided that he would still go down and pay him a visit. Geertz was not likely to be too happy either way. He pulled up a screen and tapped in a message.

I need to talk to my friend on 19 in an hour.

Talbot hesitated, wondering where exactly to send the message. He shrugged and sent it to himself. If that didn't work he would retrace his steps to Geertz' office. Talbot climbed out of the cabinet and Kerr handed him a hot cup of tea.

"Here. You look like hell by the way. You should get a shower first chance you have."

"Thanks. I don't suppose you have one of those in your cabinets too."

Kerr smiled and shook his head. "Off to 19 then?"

"Yeah, don't wait up. Seriously, I'll probably just use a podtel there too. I'll hit 10 in the morning."

"Question, Tal. You keep flitting between levels and you have even lost your watch a few times—how the hell are you getting around?"

"Trade secret."

"Pretty huge secret, man. Maybe one day you'll show me the card?"

Talbot tried not to react but Kerr snapped his fingers. "Fuck! I knew it. How do they do it? Deep background account mining or skip farthing?"

"Kerr, I don't speak nerd very well, and even if I did I can neither confirm nor deny."

"Fine, never mind. But one day…"

"One day, Kerr, I will tell you."

Talbot left and headed to the nearest lift station. Fifteen minutes later he found himself wandering the streets of 19, unsure exactly what to do next. He stood at the front of a small park near the station, watching the nighttime crowds make their way home or out to bars. He was careful to stand in a well-lit, high-traffic area. He wasn't worried about getting hassled; he just wanted Geertz, or whoever he sent, to be able to see him.

After about 20 minutes he began to get restless. He figured he could make his way down the street to where there were a bunch of food stalls and get dinner. As he stepped onto the main walkway he sensed a figure emerge from the crowd.

"He's at Cilfton's, down a block."

Talbot turned toward the sound of the voice but the man had already vanished into the crowded street.

A minute later Talbot saw the bright green neon sign that advertised the otherwise undistinguished looking bar called Clifton's. He pushed open the door and entered a dimly lit room full of people. Almost immediately a very attractive young girl wearing a fake smile and a practically nonexistent outfit took him by the elbow and steered him through the crowd towards the back. They bypassed the many booths and tables and headed down a long hallway. Talbot tensed as she gently but firmly pushed him through a swinging door. On the other side was a cramped, shabby office with a large chair, a couch with mysterious stains, and a large pull-down vid screen flashing on the wall above the chair.

Sitting in the chair was Geertz.

The girl remove herself from the room.

Talbot nodded. "Olsen's dead."

"I know," Geertz said evenly.

Talbot felt an anger rise in him that he tried to suppress. "What else did you know? Or better, what else do you know that you are not telling me?"

"Mr. Singh, there is much I know. But when it comes to this case, I think you may know much I do not. I know Aria Olsen is dead because she was shot by security forces outside a lift tube in the middle of the day. That hardly makes it a state secret. I will admit that I also knew she was part of the problem. The trouble is, and this is where you come in, Mr. Singh, I'm still not sure what the problem is."

"What about Ludwig?"

"The man she killed? An up-and-comer. Not a Treasure connection, I assure you, but someone we kept an eye on. He was successful in a number of ventures, but especially in providing people for the Mars relocation missions."

"You knew about that then?"

Geertz arched his eyebrows slightly. "Knew about what? Why is that important?"

"The kidnappings or abductions or whatever CSA was doing?"

Geertz smiled, a flash in his eyes. "Ah, yes, of course... that is the way then. I had assumed he was changing lower-level metrics to pass them off as higher-level folks. But yes, that would be far too difficult. Why not take someone already qualified but... unmotivated. How did they do it? They couldn't use a mind wipe."

"I don't know exactly, but they somehow got those girls to agree to go to Mars."

"Hmm, that would be good to know, Mr. Singh. If you could figure that out it would be invaluable."

"Why?"

"Why not? It is pretty difficult to change people's minds. I mean that literally. There are techniques to wipe a mind, but then the person is almost useless. But if you can let them keep their intellect and knowledge and yet still change their attitude about one-way exile…well, the possibilities intrigue."

"I might have a lead, I need to visit CSA."

"Good idea. That Ludwig character was in deep. I would be careful, even if he is dead."

"Yeah, he mentioned higher ups."

This caught Geertz's attention, his facade of cool slipped for a moment. "Who? Tell me!"

"I don't know, he didn't say. No one said. But he mentioned level 65. I guess this goes way up."

"Yes, to the highest levels. Solving the population issue is a pressing matter for the upper levels; they feel the pull of us lowers. It vexes them, it seems. But they are having trouble establishing a foothold on Mars. It is a difficult journey and life."

"So I hear. Still, I don't understand. This guy Ludwig promised Olsen life on 65—for what? A dozen girls? I guess I imagined the space program would be bigger than that."

"Mr. Singh, please, it is! Ludwig operated about two dozen Spacefarer agencies. He was not messing around."

Talbot felt as if the floor was falling away. Two dozen agencies like CSA? His face must have shown.

"Yes, Mr. Singh, this is much, much bigger than a dozen

coeds. We're talking about hundreds of people, maybe as many as a thousand. And if Ludwig was doing it, then who know how many others were doing it."

"We need to do something for those people."

Geertz gazed up at the ceiling. "That might be…difficult, at best. If this goes up to 65 then one can assume it goes up even higher, however high the towers rise. It will not pay to mess with those people, Mr. Singh. Not even I mess with those people. Stick to your work, Mr. Singh. Find out how they are getting people to go and we can put a stop to the trade—or do one better."

"What do you mean? If you think I'm going to help you get into this trade you should just kill me now."

Geertz looked down at Talbot and smiled. "Noble, but no worries. I have no intention of brainwashing bratty 31ers. But if there is a way to alter people's minds slightly, it would be useful down here, or lower."

"So you would sell out your own just for a few bucks?"

"Mr. Singh, please. I know you fancy yourself as salt of the earth being from 29, but recall that to me or someone below me, you might as well live in the clouds. People down below are desperate to escape. They do not have magic pass," Geertz looked meaningfully at Talbot. "One day, Mr. Singh, use that pass to go low, really low, and see what you find. People crushed, figuratively, but also sometimes almost literally, by the city above them. They would sell their soul to get out. A one-way ticket to a place uncomfortable? Heaven on earth compared to the hell they dwell in. How did you like the ceilings on eight, my friend? A little low? Ha! Skyscrapers compared to below."

"So you're telling me you can convince people to go to Mars?"

"I will have to beat them away with sticks. The problem is that they would fail the tests; their mind, their brains would betray them. A way around that..." Geertz let the possibility hang in the air.

Talbot stood there for a moment, his head pounding. "I can't promise."

"I understand. You may not even be able to find out. But trust me on one thing Talbot: if you do decide to blow this thing open, it will come down on your head. I will not be able to help you then. Best to keep this thing as quiet as you can. For my sake, yes, but mostly yours."

Talbot nodded. He had no doubt: if things did go up as far as they seemed, he would be just a minor stain on the floor. Talbot cleared his throat. "I need a place to stay tonight, and it's too late to go to the CSA now. Is there a Podtel near here?"

Geertz smiled. "We run an excellent one above this very establishment. April here will show you up. Stay as my guest, Mr. Singh."

Talbot tried to hide his surprise as the same young woman who had escorted him to the room now came through the door again, her hand held out for him to take.

"Thanks," Talbot said to Geertz. "I should know more tomorrow—or not. But either way."

"Send me another message, Mr. Singh. I won't be here."

"Of course."

April secreted Talbot to an undersized lift further down the hall. The space was tight and she casually leaned up against him as the lift slowly ascended. Talbot was pinned so he could not move, but he had to admit the situation was not exactly horrible. April was as attractive as any girl he had seen back on 29. He briefly wondered if she worked in the bar or for Geertz. He tried to keep his thoughts from straying. Best not to mess around, he told himself.

After what seemed like an eternity the lift shuddered to a stop and the doors opened into a long, deserted hallway. Down both sides were little doors about three feet tall. Each door had a keypad/screen beside it. The doors were stacked one on top the other, three high. April smiled at Talbot and walked down the hallway towards to the left. Talbot was somewhat turned around, but he felt as if they were headed away from the street. As they walked overhead lights flickered on, sensing their presence. After passing what Talbot guessed were a hundred or more doors, they finally came to the end of the hallway.

Talbot noticed the doors here were somewhat wider. April read his expression and laughed pleasantly. "This is the presidential suite area, the luxury tubetel pods."

Talbot smiled. April took his hand and pressed it against a screen by the lowest door. The door gave a small click and gently swung open.

"It's keyed to your metrics. They have nicer ones up top, but these are clean," she said matter-of-factly.

Talbot bent over and looked inside. "Looks nice enough."

There was an awkward moment. He wasn't sure if he was supposed to crawl in now but he wanted to find food first. He assumed they did not have room service. April smiled and with an assured grace took his hand and kissed him full on the lips.

Talbot automatically pushed her away. She looked annoyed at the rejection.

"Sorry," he apologized.

"It's okay. If you don't like girls we have plenty of guys."

Talbot chuckled. "No, no, not that. Look, you are very pretty and everything, but I just saw the last woman I slept with get shot, right in front of me, so…"

"Consider me your rebound then," April said, just as if she was explaining the metric keyed door.

Talbot looked at her and bit his upper lip. A thought occurred to him. "Will you get in trouble if I say no?"

April laughed. "Hell no! Not like that. I work for Mr. Geertz. I do lots of things for him. I'm not a full time whore, but again if that's your speed, I can get one. Maybe something a bit skankier?"

Talbot rolled his eyes. "I was just checking. Sorry if I insulted you. Truth is, I'm kinda shaky on all this."

"Sex?"

"No, not that. I've got that down alright. No, the whole Treasure thing. I don't want to cross the wrong people."

April leaned against the opposite wall of doors and sighed. "You're over thinking it." Her demeanor changed, she was no longer trying to play a part, or perhaps, Talbot thought, she was merely playing a new part.

"No, I'm being cautious."

"Whatever. Look, I'm offering. It's not a big deal. But if the answer is no and you don't want a boy, then I got shit I can do."

Talbot laughed. "I liked it better when you were trying. Mind if I ask you something first?"

"Fire away."

"You from 19?"

"Naw, from 12. You? I figure you're from upper someplace."

"29."

"You slumming then?"

"Working."

"For Geertz?"

Talbot hesitated. Was he? "Not exactly. Well, not really at all. I work for people up on 29, trying to help them find a girl."

"She run away?"

"Abducted."

"Maybe."

"Maybe what?"

"Maybe. Maybe not. She from 29?"

"No. Her Mom was but she moved up to 31. The girl was at the uni."

"So how do you know she got abducted?"

"She was with friends, at a bar."

"You protocol?"

"No, assist."

"Huh, little young for that. And it shows. That girl, goes to a bar and disappears."

"Taken."

"Disappears. Best way to go. Plenty of people know you leave, that you're gone. That's how I would do it, to make sure no one comes after you."

"Well, didn't work that way, did it? I'm after her."

"She leave a note, ransom demands, anything left behind?"

Talbot smiled. "You work the assist too?"

"Like I said, I'm not some dumb whore."

"What are you then?"

April fingered a necklace she was wearing. "Just someone trying to get by."

"Why did you leave 12?"

"Why stay? There's worse but there's a lot better."

"How far up you been?" Talbot asked.

She closed her eyes as if trying to remember. "Dunno exactly, could be someplace in the 60s."

"No shit?"

She opened her eyes again. "Impressed?" She laughed. "Please. Like I said, I get by."

"Ever think about going legit?"

"Mister, everything I do is legit, okay?" She pressed a finger into his chest. "I don't need saving, Talbot Singh, but I wouldn't mind spending some time with you and getting a good fuck out of it." She pressed both hands up against him.

Talbot smiled. "How can I resist that kind of come on?"

Sometime later the two of them were lying on the thin mattress that filled the tiny room or pod. Low recessed lights gave the room an orange glow. April rolled over and pulled a screen down.

"Eight already? I better get going."

"That bad eh?"

April laughed. "Naw, you were good, baby. I guess you do like girls well enough. I just need to get back to work."

"Doing?"

She gave him a playful slap on the chest. "Not that! Whatever Geertz wants."

"I'm sure he won't mind."

"Don't be. He doesn't exactly know I'm here."

Talbot raised his head. "He didn't tell you to, uh…"

April shook her head. "Like I said, I'm not that kind of girl. But, I am," she said, lifting herself up enough to slip her blouse and skirt back on, "a real girl, Talbot Singh. And I have flesh and blood."

"I'll say."

She looked at him and then laughed.

"Hey, one more favor?" Talbot asked. She looked at him skeptically. "Can you recommend a good place to eat cheap? I'm starving."

"Sure, baby. Come on, put on your pants and I'll drop you off at the best Dahl cart on 19."

By the time Talbot crawled back into his luxury tube he passed out without even getting undressed and fell into a deep and dreamless sleep. A void of nothingness.

CHAPTER FIFTEEN

When he woke the pod lights were slowly changing from deep blue to bright red orange. A low, persistent beeping tickled his ears. He looked at the screen that had come down above his head and saw that it was already almost 9:00 a.m.

His head felt remarkably clear as he pulled himself out into the hallway. Moments later he was on the street, which was full of people busy going to work, going about their lives. How often had he stood on streets like this, watching people? Had he ever really just stopped and looked. What were they so busy doing, he wondered? Working, getting paid, eating their wages, and crapping their wages. All of it a mad scramble to get…where?

Where had he ever been? A week ago he would have said level 45 or some such non-destination. Now he had been to the edge, to the outer limits of the city. But even that, where was that? What was it? He had been so overwhelmed, so scared, he had barely glimpsed what outside really was. He could not bear the thought of leaving his city behind, his parents, his friends—his world. But, in the back of his mind, he was forming an understanding of how one might. How one might want to leave the city, even leave the world, and go someplace, anyplace—even to your own demise on a cold, barren planet millions of miles away.

Would he spend a year in a small tin can just to get to someplace even worse? As Talbot looked around he smiled. The city may not be a tin can, but how different was it? Even on 29 all one had to do was look up and be instantly reminded of how confined you were. How limited you were. Maybe on Mars or Europa you could look up and see the endless plains of Mars. Or stars. Or Jupiter slowly turning in awesome majesty. No matter how far up he went, Talbot realized, he would always be looking up at a ceiling.

He sighed. Maybe Geertz was right. Who knew? Right now he just wanted to figure out how to get Jahn back. If he could. If she was still alive. After that…well, it was a big city. He would figure out something.

He took the lift to 10. At this hour the car was almost empty. It put Talbot at ease; he was pretty sure no one was following him, although he knew the metrics on his watch would register the change in level. Somewhere, someone or something would register that.

In many ways 10 was worse than eight. The ceiling certainly was no higher. But more than that it was the architecture; this level was newer than eight, but the buildings seemed older, cheaper and the buildings lent an air of depression.

Once out of the station building and onto the inevitable market street, Talbot checked his watch. The address Kerr had given him was fairly far off. It stood to reason that it would be at the edge. Kerr had told him that ships launched from just outside the city so having direct access to the outside would be essential.

Talbot hopped on a subway and within fifteen minutes was in a quiet, almost deserted neighborhood lined with similar dull-fronted buildings. They were almost comical in their blandness and similarity. Beige stucco stone with small black windows set high above the street seemed to be the area's general style. He wondered if it was meant to be cheap or if it was meant to camouflage the agency. They screamed government buildings to Talbot.

He walked through the only doorway that he could see. Inside was a small waiting area dominated by a large desk where a thin, young man sat. Arrayed in front of him were five hard plastic chairs: two in one row, three in the next. A half dead plant stood sentinel in the corner.

The young man looked up as Talbot entered, hastily flicking away a small screen from his watch. He plastered on a smile and look of eagerness. Talbot felt himself relax. He could work with this guy.

"Hello, how can I help you?"

"Is this the Launch Processing Center?"

"That is housed here, yes."

Talbot felt some of that relaxed feeling ebb away. The kid may have looked eager, but he certainly had the governmental non-answer down.

"Great. I'm looking for some information on someone."

The helpful expression vanished from the young man's face. "Sorry, we can't talk about personnel."

"I get that, but it's kind of important."

"You can put in a request for information file."

"I already did that."

The young man tilted his head. "Did you get a reply?"

"Yes. No match."

There was silence. The expression on the man's face was one of utter confusion. "So, that means the person doesn't work here."

"Look, uh...?"

"Louis."

"Louis. I'm looking for a girl. Possibly a recruit. "

"A recruit?"

"A spacefarer."

"Okay. But your query came back not found?"

"Yes. Look, she may not be here under her real name."

"Impossible. We use metrics to—"

"I know, I know," Talbot said impatiently. He felt the conversation slipping away but did not want to say too much.

"Look, how many of these folks do you get in each week?"

"That is classified," Louis said nervously. He could tell where this was going and he did not want to start a fight.

"Really? Okay, then let me guess. Ten?"

Louis did not respond but looked up, meaningfully.

"Twenty?"

Again he looked up. Talbot swore to himself.

"Thirty? Fifty? Sweet, fifty. Wow. Okay, about two weeks ago did you get a girl—"

"Sir."

"Just hear me out. Young...your age about, average build, black hair, almond eyes, smart, cute."

The young man smiled then caught himself and frowned.

Talbot chose his words carefully. "I know you can't tell me

anything, Louis, but let me tell you some stuff, okay?"

Louis nodded, as if afraid to speak.

"Jahn is the daughter of a friend of mine. About two weeks ago she disappeared from the uni on 31, Atlanta. All I need to know is if she is okay, or even alive, okay?"

Louis had a puzzled look on his face. "Jahn?"

"Yes, Jahn."

Louis studied Talbot for a moment and then shook his head. "Sorry, even if I could tell you, there would not be anyone here by that name."

"Okay, but that's just it. She may be here under a different name."

"Not possible, like I said."

"I know, but listen: what if?" Talbot felt himself grasping at straws. "Look, maybe I have the name wrong."

"Friend of the family?"

"I'm an assist, but yeah, I went to school with her mom. Look," Talbot lowered his voice and leaned in, "give me a sign. Something."

Louis sat back, his face a mixture of worry and concern.

"I can't, sir. There is nothing I can tell you. Now, if you'll have a seat," Louis nodded meaningfully at the two rows of plastic seats.

Talbot looked at the chairs then back at Louis, who was slowly nodding. Talbot, not knowing whether to feel dread or anticipation, slowly lowered himself onto the edge of one seat. Louis pulled up a small screen from the desk and turned it around. Floating above the desk the screen read On Break. Louis got up and went through a door behind the desk and vanished into the back.

Five minutes went by and Louis was still not back. But, Talbot thought, the protocol had not come for him either, so there was that. Then the door opened. A slight young woman with long, black hair and almond eyes, wearing an orange jumpsuit cautiously peered out.

He had found Jahn.

The girl slid into the room, closing the door quickly behind her. Talbot stood, his heart racing.

"Ja—"

She put her finger to her lips and shook her head. "Hi," she said pleasantly but unsmiling. "I'm Rachel. Louis sent me out here. He said you wanted to talk to me?"

Talbot's mouth went dry. He cleared his throat but his voice still sounded ragged. "Right. Is there a place near here we can go talk?" He assumed the waiting room was bugged.

She nodded. "Coffee bar. Near here. Come on."

She led him through the building and once outside he tried to talk again. But again she shushed him and they walked in silence, with Talbot almost bursting. They walked straight past one coffee bar then another. When they reached what looked like an apartment lobby she grabbed his arm and quickly dragged him inside, where she slammed him against a wall.

"I can shove your nose right up your face, Mister. Kill you quick," she announced, her hand inches from Talbot's face. "Who the fuck are you and what do you want?"

He raised his hands, palms out. "I'm Talbot Singh, an assist from 29. Your grandmother asked me to find you. It is you, Jahn, right?"

She did not answer and drew her hand back. Talbot felt his stomach drop. Then she paused. "Did you tell her you found me?"

"No, I just found you."

"Who else knows?"

"People know. There's a guy—"

"Uh-huh. Sorry, Mister."

"He's in the Treasure. If I don't come back he'll know I found you and then he'll come get you no matter what," Talbot said in rush.

Jahn looked at him with a tilted head. "Why would this guy come get me?"

"Because he thinks you have something he wants. Something with metrics?"

She relaxed her hold slightly. With all the force he could summon, Talbot swung out his leg, cutting her down. She pulled at his shirt. He grabbed her right arm and by the time she hit the floor, knocking the breath out of her, he had her arm pinned at a painful angle behind her back. She tried to speak, but her lungs were gulping for breath. Talbot waited, counted to 10, and then relaxed the pressure on her arm . She did not struggle.

"Sorry about that, princess, but we need to talk. You ready to talk or not?"

She nodded. He let go of her arm and stood up. She lay on the floor for a minute and then slowly pushed herself up. Her hair was a mess but she was not hurt.

"No coffee bar then, okay?" Talbot said, trying to sound less freaked out than he was. "Is there a place nearby, one where we can talk?"

She nodded and pointed out the window to a pub across the street. "Lunch rush isn't for another hour," she spat out.

Talbot opened the door. "After you."

The place was a restaurant, fairly nice. It must have done good business being so close to the space agency offices. Talbot steered them towards the back, near the kitchen. He figured it would be noisier here once the rush started, allow them to talk without being overheard.

Jahn sat down across from Talbot in the tiny booth. She seemed to have changed her attitude. Talbot figured she had meant to kill him to prevent him from telling anyone about her. Now with that option off the table, he could see her trying to figure out another way to silence him. He mentally tucked that away as a chit to cash in.

"Who are you really?" Jahn asked.

Talbot flicked his wrist and his license popped up on a floating screen. "Talbot Singh, assist, level 29. It's all there in the metrics."

Jahn flicked the screen away with her fingers. "Metrics," she said, flatly.

"What about them?" Talbot asked.

Jahn ignored him. "So what do you want exactly?"

"Nothing much. I think I have it already. But I do have questions."

"I bet."

"Jahn," Talbot saw her flinch, "people are worried about you."

"I know it, but that's not important right now."

"Why not? Tell me what's going on."

Jahn studied him for a moment. "How do I know who you

are? You say you know my mom?"

"She a family friend. Your grandmum hired me to figure out what happened to your grandfather. And then when you went missing…"

Jahn narrowed her eyes. "So prove it. Tell me something about my mum most people wouldn't know."

"Like what?"

"Her favorite food."

"I didn't date her."

"Okay, then, about Gran. What's covering her couch?"

"Her couch? Why would I know that?"

Jahn crossed her arms and tilted her head. "You've been in there, if you say you are who you are, right? Look, I don't know who you are but if you're here to kill me, do it quick. Otherwise let me get on with what's left of my life." She stood up. "Tell your Treasure people to fuck off. I'll be gone before they can finishing pissing."

She turned and walked towards the door as the image popped into Talbot's head.

"Wait!" he called after her. "A zebra skin. That's what's on her couch."

Jahn stopped. She came back and sat down, a curious look on her face. "Okay, so maybe you are someone, but doesn't mean much anyway. Tell me what you know so far and I'll see if you know how much trouble you're in."

"Me?"

"Yes, you."

"I'm not in trouble."

Jahn stared at him impassively for a moment. "If you're not

scared then you don't know shit."

"I'm not scared," Talbot said. "But I know there's some strange stuff going down and that people up there, way up there, have their hand in it."

Jahn smiled. "Go on."

"Okay. I think that there are orgs out there that are, somehow, taking young people from higher levels and making them or convincing them to go to Mars or Europa, despite the fact it's a one-way ticket. I met one of the people involved. She was protocol. And saw her with another, who she killed. I don't know who else is involved, but I bet it goes way up to the top and I bet they aren't worried about me."

Jahn smiled and sat back, visibly relaxed.

"You have the basic outline. Look, I'm glad I didn't kill you. That would have been messy. And unnecessary because you're already dead. You think there is some sort of connection higher up? You have no idea, do you?"

Talbot did not reply. He did not know what to say.

"What does Treasure want with me?"

"They want to know how the girls were made to go to Mars."

Jahn exhaled a long breath. "You want to know how? Me too, me too. I don't really know. Look, I'm not who they want. I can tell you who we dealt with, maybe he knows."

"We?"

Jahn smiled. "Good catch. Yeah, we. Granddad and me."

Talbot felt numb. "What?"

"Grandad and me," Jahn repeated, somewhat forlornly.

"Jahn, I know. Deesee told me about you and him. If you

don't want to talk about it—"

Jahn laughed, a little too loud. "You talked to Deesee? How is she?"

"Fine. Worried."

"She was crazy. I think she was in love with me, you know? But yeah, I told her a lot of shit."

"Like what?"

"About me and Granddad. Look, I was scared. Still am. Deesee liked me; I think she was jealous. Me and Granddad always going off. I couldn't tell her what was really going on, right? So I made shit up, told her he was harassing me. You know, nasty stuff."

"He wasn't?"

"Fuck no! The old man treated me like gold…well, that way." She went very quiet and looked down at the table, as if it held answers. "What he did was… I almost wish all he was doing would'a been that kind of shit."

"What did he do?" Talbot asked.

"He was always nice to me, you know? As a little girl, his favorite. Bought me stuff. Stupid stuff. He encouraged me too. Wanted me to go to uni. I guess it was part of a plan. I dunno." She stared into space, contemplating the thought. "Anyways, once I got to the uni he started visiting me. The first one, I didn't know what he was doing, I swear. He asked about a girl. Did I know her? I thought I knew her from class." Words tumbled out, as if in release. "He had me invite her over and then I thought, you know, that maybe he was a perv but…," Jahn started to cry but quickly brought herself under control. "He wasn't a perv, okay? But he had this guy with him, and they gave her a shot or something, and the guy took her away. I was super freaked out. I told him I would go to the protocol, I would tell everyone, but he talked me down. Kept telling me the girl was okay and that I was now an accomplice anyway. I made him tell me exactly what was going on. I needed to know, but once he did I realized I had no real choice."

"What do you mean?"

"I was in for good, you know? I knew enough to be dangerous. I had to play along to survive."

"What was he doing?"

"Taking the girls down here to the Mars mission. They did something with the metrics. You know, switched them. That's the easy part. Deesee could even do it. She did do it."

"Deesee was involved?"

"No, no, she didn't know anything. Like I said, I had to lie just to get her off the trail."

"Okay, so they switched metrics, but you still have the girls. Wouldn't they talk, try to get out of going?"

"That's the part that isn't clear. The guy who worked with Granddad would take the girls to a clinic and a few hours later they would come out, convinced they were really whatever new metric they'd been given and that they really, really wanted to go to Mars."

"How?"

"I don't know."

"Okay, then what?"

"They'd bring them down here. The preflight stuff is easy, less than a week. I'm only a day away from leaving myself. Most of the stuff here is all psych and health evals."

"What about the girl they found?"

"Rose or whatever her name was? Yeah, she was a bad one. I guess the stuff the guy does isn't 100 percent for everyone. When she died, that's when I began to think about how to get out."

Talbot smiled as he put it together. "So you faked your own kidnapping."

Jahn nodded.

"Changed your metrics. Or Deesee did and you didn't need the voodoo guy 'cause you think going to Mars will put you out of reach."

Jahn nodded.

"Seems extreme. Once your granddad was dead couldn't you have just faded away?"

Jahn shook her head. "The guy who helped knew me and probably others. Granddad's contact, what's her name...Olsen."

"Of course," Talbot said, more to himself.

"Besides, I couldn't stick around...especially after I killed him."

Talbot felt his heart miss a beat. "Who? Your granddad?"

Jahn bit her lip and nodded.

"Why?"

"We had done what, like 12 girls? When was it going to stop? I didn't know how else to stop it, man. So I shot him. I planned it out. I was pretty careful. I got Deesee to help me with a new metric and some other stuff."

"Like the Treasure card?"

Jahn smiled. "Yeah, thought that would throw them off the scent long enough."

"But it didn't."

Her smile faded.

"The card was out of date. It's why I got caught up with this whole thing. It's why Treasure is interested in your guy."

"Fuck."

"It's okay, Jahn."

"No, fuck! Deesee and Jessica. Fuck!"

"Calm down, I think they're okay. I can contact Deesee, tell her to cover herself and Jessica. She's pretty good, despite the card screw up. Jahn, look at me—they're okay. I saw Olsen kill Ludwig."

Jahn looked puzzled.

"He was the connection between 31 and the upper levels."

"Fuck!"

"But he's dead now." Talbot held back that Ludwig told Olsen he had called someone higher up. Talbot hoped that whatever Ludwig knew about Jahn, Deesee, and Jessica had died with him.

"Shit! This is so fucked up now."

"Listen, Jahn, it's not. I think I have a way we can fix this—all of this. But I'm going to need your help. I need you to talk about this."

"What do you mean?"

"Record a video or an audio—either one—explaining where the girls are. Do you know their new names?"

"I think I can remember them all. But, I can't do that. They'll get me, I know."

"No, they won't. I'll hold onto it. Or better yet, you can time synch it in the cloud and it won't come out until you are days out. They can't pull you back."

Jahn shook her head. "They'll find me either way."

"But not if you deliver it as Jahn. No one knows who you are now right?

"You do, and Deesee."

"That's it, right?"

"I guess."

"I'll do you one better. If you tell me the name of the guy, I'll pass it to Treasure. In return I'll ask that they kill Jahn."

Jahn smiled slightly. "You mean the old me, right."

"Of course."

"And my mom and grandma?"

"I can tell them, or not. Your choice."

"I have to think about that. You can make this all happen?"

"I promise."

"When?"

"Right now. We'll find a store, get you a T-shirt and find some generic background. Could be anywhere. I can have Treasure scrub the video so it can't be traced." Talbot wasn't sure if that was even possible, but he did not want to give Jahn time to change her mind. If she left now she might never come back.

She nodded. "Okay."

The next morning Talbot stood outside the lift station on 19 again. He waited a few minutes and then began to walk down the street. He was not surprised to see April fall in step.

"Was 10 good?"

"Very."

"Good. Go to the 130 block here, building 17, office eight."

"One-thirty, 17, eight."

"Beauty." April grabbed his arm and kissed him on the cheek. She smiled and then melted into the crowd.

Through the large glass windows that lined the hallways he could see number eight was clean, well lit, spacious, but empty. He let himself in. As the door closed the windows behind him became glistening white walls. Neat trick, he thought.

Geertz walked in from a door set in the back of the room. "I hear you have good news for me, Mr. Singh."

"Yes," Talbot said evenly. "But I need a favor."

Geertz cocked his head. "Mr. Singh, the information you hopefully have is, itself, payment for a favor."

"I know, but I have even more information so I want another favor. Not for myself, of course."

"Go on."

"I found Jahn, as you might have guessed. And she told me lots of stuff. She is going to release a video about what was going on."

"Most unwise."

"Hear me out. So I need you to kill her metrics."

"Why?"

"Because Jahn no longer exists anyway. She's gone away and become someone new."

"Really?"

"I can't tell you anything else, although I suppose you could find out pretty quickly. But I need you to kill Jahn off so people, you know, won't come looking for her."

"You want me to throw her watch down an elevator shaft?"

Geertz smiled.

Talbot allowed himself a small smile. "Yes."

"And what do you give me in return."

"A heads up. Jahn has a vid where she explains everything she knows: mainly that the girls are on Mars and who they are. I thought you might like to know, in case that messes up any of your plans."

Geertz was quiet for a moment. "It might, Mr.Singh. They will, no doubt, sharpen their psych evals on future volunteers."

"But your people want to go, right?"

"Yes, Mr. Singh, yes they do, which might help. I applaud your concern and your noble effort to put things right. It complicates matters, but it does not make them impossible. Consider it done then; the ghost of Jahn will die sometime soon."

"Good. We'll hold the vid for a few days anyway."

"And now the real thing, Mr. Singh."

"Yeah, the guy. Henry Laine, MD. Level 36, Tower 1126. Jahn couldn't tell me the method used, but I figure you'll be able to offer him some sort of deal. At least for his sake I hope you can. After the vid he'll be walking dead I would guess."

"And you?"

"I'm as clean as I can be. I'll be careful."

"I hope for your sake you are, Mr. Singh. You have proved to be a valuable asset." Geertz gave a little bow. "Keep the card, Mr. Singh. Be judicious about its use. And in the future I might call on your services again."

It was a statement, not a question. Talbot nodded.

"Thank you," Geertz said and left.

A few days later Talbot sat at the counter of Kerr's store. The nanobots in the sign were making crude, rude animations. A vid screen floated in back of the little store as Kerr he pulled out several boxes of watches.

"You sure you want to trade in, Tal? I know I said you hang on to them too long, but I mean, it's only been a few days."

"Yeah, I want to shake this one."

"Well, look at these." Kerr pulled out some of the watches. "So I trust things wrapped up?"

"About to. Is it noon yet?"

"Ten past."

"They've had an hour...ah, there it is. Look at the screen, Kerr. Turn up the volume."

Breaking news had replaced the football broadcast. A reporter was talking breathlessly. "The allegations in this video are astounding. If true they could expose high-level corruption. It also identifies 15 girls thought to be dead who are now assumed to be working under aliases on the Mars mission."

The screen changed to Jahn in a white T-shirt and dark glasses, her black hair pulled back and hidden under a bright red knit cap, standing against a grey wall. She spoke slowly, as if reading from a screen.

"My name is Jahn Stovall. I worked with my grandfather, Mr. Jay Mill, to kidnap 15 girls from Atlanta Uni over the course of three years. These girls are not dead. They were placed on missions to Mars and all, as far as I know, are still there. The only exception was

Rose Roberts, who was found on level eight. My granddad never told me anything about who he worked for. I do have the names of the girls as they are now metrixed. They are Alicia Carpenter..."

The broadcast switched back to the reporter. "All of this is unconfirmed, but we do have a report from protocol that Ms. Jahn Singleton killed herself two days ago, having thrown herself onto a subway track."

"I'll take this one, Kerr," Talbot said quietly.

Kerr turned, his jaw slack. "Okay, sure. Holy shit, Tal. What have you done?"

"Nothing. And if you know what's healthy, you've never asked me that."

Kerr went white but nodded. "Yeah, of course. I know."

"See you around."

"Sure, Tal. And hey, sorry you never got to find Jahn before she killed herself."

Talbot smiled and left. He had one more stop to make.

He swallowed hard as he buzzed the flat. A click and the door was open. He went inside the building, up to the apartment, and knocked. Mrs. Mill opened the door, behind her was Jessica.

Talbot looked at the two women. "I'm so sorry to hear about Jahn..."

THE END

D H Richards teaches at a small Southern Liberal Arts College. Levels is his second novel, the first being the fantasy The Hare, the Bow & the Girl: Book One: Dream of the Lepus. He grew up in the foothills of the Blue Ridge mountains in Virginia.

Made in the USA
Middletown, DE
03 May 2017